"How close were you to the car?"

"I'd gotten in and realized I hadn't closed the trunk. I was behind the car when it just—" Bellamy broke off, the disbelief still clear in her eyes. "When it just exploded."

"We're going to take a look at it but first I need Alex to sniff the rest of the cars that are still here so we can get these people out of here. Can you wait for me?"

"Where else am I going to go?"

For reasons Donovan couldn't explain, he sensed there was something more in her comment. Something that went well beyond a car bomb or the shaky aftereffects of surviving a crime.

Something terrible had taken the light out of her beautiful gray eyes.

And he was determined to find out why.

***

**The Coltons of Shadow Creek:
Only family can keep you safe...**

COLTON
K-9 COP

———

ADDISON FOX

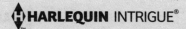

HARLEQUIN INTRIGUE®

Special thanks and acknowledgment to Addison Fox
for her contribution to The Coltons of Shadow Creek miniseries.

For Max

You came into my life when I least expected it and have colored my world with puppy cuddles, cookie (mis)adventures and joy.

Always joy.

ISBN-13: 978-1-335-72132-7

Colton K-9 Cop

Copyright © 2017 by Harlequin Books S.A.

Recycling programs
for this product may
not exist in your area.

Printed in U.S.A.

A12007 002507

Addison Fox is a lifelong romance reader, addicted to happy-ever-afters. After discovering she found as much joy writing about romance as she did reading it, she's never looked back. Addison lives in New York with an apartment full of books, a laptop that's rarely out of sight and a wily beagle who keeps her running. You can find her at her home on the web at www.addisonfox.com or on Facebook (Facebook.com/addisonfoxauthor) and Twitter (@addisonfox).

Books by Addison Fox

Harlequin Intrigue

The Coltons of Shadow Creek

Colton K-9 Cop

Harlequin Romantic Suspense

The Coltons of Shadow Creek

Cold Case Colton

The Coltons of Texas

Colton's Surprise Heir

Dangerous in Dallas

Silken Threats
Tempting Target
The Professional
The Royal Spy's Redemption

House of Steele

The Paris Assignment
The London Deception
The Rome Affair
The Manhattan Encounter

The Adair Affairs

Secret Agent Boyfriend

Visit the Author Profile page at Harlequin.com.

CAST OF CHARACTERS

Bellamy Reeves—Facing the holiday season alone, Bellamy's focused on keeping her attention on her job at Lone Star Pharmaceutical. When she's the recipient of a mysterious email, she's fired and nearly blown up. Is the sexy K-9 cop who comes to her rescue a protector or an investigator seeking information on what she might know?

Donovan Colton—The adopted son of the powerful Colton family, Donovan is most content when he's solving crimes with his K-9 partner, Alex. The latest mystery at Lone Star Pharmaceutical puts him directly in contact with the most enticing woman he's ever met—but is she what she seems?

Alex—Donovan's K-9 partner, the five-year-old black Lab is loyal and an excellent judge of character.

Sutton Taylor—Founder of Lone Star Pharmaceutical, he has the town of Whisperwood, Texas, in his palm. Is it possible he's using his influence to create illegal sales for LSP's most needed drugs?

Jensen Taylor—Heir apparent to Lone Star Pharmaceutical, Jensen's in possession of a secret that could shake the foundations of his family.

Maggie Corgan (formerly Reeves)—The belle of Whisperwood, Bellamy's younger sister escaped her responsibilities to the family after their father was injured. What secret is she hiding?

Sally Borne—Recently hired to run Human Resources at Lone Star Pharmaceutical, she's cold and calculating and knows more about the inner workings of LSP than anyone can imagine.

Chief Archer Thompson—Chief of the Whisperwood PD, Archer thinks Bellamy's innocent until proven guilty, but can't quite shake his doubts about her. Is she an innocent victim or a woman who's setting everything in motion for her own benefit?

Prologue

Five years ago

She held the garland loosely in her hand as she slowly unwound the bright gold in steady, even rows. Turn by turn, the empty green branches filled with the shiny, vivid color as Bellamy Reeves enjoyed watching her handiwork come to life.

Her parents had asked her to work the store this evening, their annual holiday event with the local men's club a highlight of their year. She'd been happy to do it, the familiar work of managing the counter and ringing up purchases at Whisperwood's only corner store something she'd been doing since childhood. It was a far cry from her work in finance at Lone Star Pharmaceutical but it kept her in touch with her roots and she enjoyed it.

Add on that it gave her a shot at stringing up the decorations just to her personal specifications, and it was a job she was happy to take on.

Maggie had teased her about risking spinsterhood if she were willing to work the family store on a holiday Saturday night and Bellamy had ignored her. Her sister was fond of quoting all the pithy reasons Bellamy was doomed to a lonely existence and she'd learned to ignore it.

Or, if not ignore it, at least stop caring about it so much.

Her sister was the resident beauty queen of Whisperwood, Texas. She'd had men wrapped around her finger basically since she'd crawled out of the womb and had learned to drape herself over their arms not much longer after that.

Bellamy was different.

She wasn't afraid of men. Nor was she afraid of dating or putting herself out there. She dated regularly but just hadn't found anyone who interested her. Or made her feel special.

She'd spent her life observing her parents' marriage and knew that was the type of love and companionship she sought. A deep, abiding commitment that bonded the two of them together.

Tonight was a perfect example.

Although it was the men's club event, both her parents enjoyed the evening in equal measure. It was *nice*, she mused as she dug in a large plastic container for another string of garland. And while the event might seem simple or unimportant—a dinner dance at the Whisperwood Lodge—it was something they looked forward to and talked about all year long.

The bell over the front door of the store jingled and Bellamy eyed the entrance as a well-built man pushed his way in, a puppy cradled in his arms. Her father was fairly laid-back about the store, but since they sold food, animals were forbidden unless in service. "I'm sorry, sir, but the dog needs to stay outside."

Dark brows slashed over even darker eyes and the

guy juggled the black Lab pup from one well-formed arm to another, his biceps flexing as he shifted the limp bundle. "Believe it or not, he's a service dog. In training," the guy quickly added before reaching into his back pocket and pulling out a badge. "I'm with the Austin PD. I'm his handler."

The sight of the puppy—and the sudden delight she didn't need to kick them out—had her crossing the store to greet them. "He's sweet."

"And sick, I think. He's not very energetic and he won't eat."

"Oh." She reached out to lay a hand on the small head, the fur silky soft over the bony ridges of his skull. He was small, but the large paws that hung over the man's forearms indicated the puppy would be a big guy once fully grown.

"I wanted to pick up some chicken and rice and hoped you'd have what I needed."

"Would you believe me if I told you I had both already cooked in the stockroom?"

"Seriously?"

"Yep. They're my bland leftovers from lunch that I brought along in some vague attempt to offset Christmas cookie consumption."

Although he wasn't inappropriate, his eyes drifted over her body before settling back on her face. "You're dieting?"

Heat burned a path where he'd gazed, that steady appreciation lighting a fire. "I prefer to think of it as holiday calorie management. A goal I'm failing at miserably, seeing as how the bland chicken and even blander rice were horrible."

"Why not toss it?"

"Some vague notion of trying again tomorrow. You know—" she waved a hand as she headed for the back of the store "—to make up for the pizza I ate in its place today."

A hearty laugh followed her through the swinging door into the stockroom and she beelined for the fridge and the leftovers.

Her father's store carried all the basic necessities of a convenience store and boasted a fairly hearty kitchen out front to accommodate the breakfast and lunch crowds who buzzed in for coffee and portable meals. She'd nuke the chicken and rice out at the counter and be able to keep an eye on the front door at the same time.

She could also keep an eye on Officer Hottie.

Wow, the man was good-looking. His body, evident beneath the long-sleeved black T-shirt that seemed sculpted to his shoulders, was strong without being imposing. And the way he cradled the dog had pretty much put her ovaries on high alert.

He was hot *and* a dog lover. Did it get much better?

She pushed through the stockroom door, only to see the back of the guy's head disappear through the front exit. Spears of disappointment layered over the lingering heat until she saw him bend over through the glass, his small charge quivering before him on the sidewalk. She raced to the counter and grabbed a few bottles of water, then headed for the miserable little puppy getting sick on the front parking lot.

"Is he okay?"

The guy glanced up from where he crouched on the ground, his hand on the small black back. "I think so. Or he will be."

She passed down a bottle of water, touched when the guy twisted it open and poured some into his palm. "Come on, Alex. Here you go."

The small head bent toward that cupped hand, the sound of his tongue lapping drifting toward her in the cool night air.

"Poor baby." She didn't miss the three brightly colored plastic pieces that lay in the pile of vomit. "Legos strike again."

"What?"

She pointed toward the small pile. "Looks like a blue vase holding a single plastic flower and a two-piece."

Officer Hottie's gaze zeroed in on the offending irritants, his voice gruff. "Just the pieces my niece mentioned were missing from her masterpiece before we sat down to dinner."

He poured more water into his hand and the Lab lapped it up, the trauma of his ordeal fading as his natural eagerness returned.

"He's looking better already." Bellamy opened the second bottle and poured it over the sidewalk, erasing the evidence and washing the Lego blocks aside. She'd come out later and pick them up with a broom.

Or planned to, until the guy pulled out a hanky from his back pocket and cleaned up the plastic, tossing the entire package into the trash. "That'll teach me to let dog or child out of my sight together again."

"That's wise." She couldn't resist his rueful grin or the clear relief in his dark eyes. Suddenly conscious of standing there staring at him, she shifted her gaze toward Alex's sweet face and the tongue that lolled out the side of his mouth. "Why don't you come back in and we can give him the food?"

"If you're sure?"

She smiled at that. "I'm certainly not going to eat it, no matter how many vows I make to myself. It'll be nice to see it go to a more appreciative recipient. Plus, he should probably go easy on dinner based on his recent Lego binge. The bland food won't hurt him."

The guy followed her back inside and she picked up the discarded container to warm up the leftovers.

"Would you mind if I came behind the counter and washed up?" He pointed to the sink beside her.

"Come on."

"Then I can introduce myself properly and shake your hand." He settled the puppy on the ground, issuing a series of commands that had the small body sitting up straight. The little guy tried to move, his butt squirming on the floor a few times, but ultimately gave in to the firm tone and the unyielding command by sitting where he was told.

"He's good. How old is he?"

"About ten weeks."

"And he can listen already?"

"'Sit' is about all he can listen to, but he's coming along." Hands clean, the guy turned the full force of his attention on her. For the briefest moment, Bellamy could have sworn she saw stars, the sky around his face glowing brighter than the gold of the garland. Quelling the ridiculous impression, she focused on the moment and not making an ass out of herself, especially when that warm, slightly damp palm closed around hers.

"I'm Donovan Colton."

Colton?

The Coltons were well known in Texas; several branches of the family were scattered across the Hill

Country. She thought she knew the entire family who lived in Whisperwood, but hadn't placed Donovan when he'd walked in.

Shaking off the sudden awareness when she realized she was standing there, staring at the man, she quickly shook his hand. "Bellamy Reeves."

"Thank you, Bellamy. I appreciate the help."

"I'm happy to help. And I'm glad the little guy's okay."

The microwave pinged and she pulled the food out, then transferred it to a paper plate before handing it over. The moment was oddly domestic, Donovan's close proximity and their joint actions to put food together for the puppy surprisingly intimate.

The bell over the store entrance pinged and she went to help her customer. One of the high school coaches, who came in regularly for his nightly dinner of soda and a meatball sub seemed unphased by the addition of a puppy behind the counter.

"Hey, Bell. Haven't seen you in a few weeks."

"I'm helping my parents out tonight. They're out cutting a rug at the men's club event."

"You doing well?"

"Yep. We're closing out a busy year at work."

"How's Magnolia doing?"

It happened often enough, she wasn't sure why she was surprised any longer. The small talk as a method to ask about her sister. The pretend friendliness that was really just a fishing expedition.

"Maggie's good. She had a hot date tonight so she abandoned me in favor of a night of dinner and dancing."

Bellamy handed over the sub, not surprised when

the coach's face fell. And while she'd not-so-delicately delivered news he obviously didn't want to hear, it didn't make the facts of Maggie's plans any less true. The besotted coach paid and was on his way out without saying much more.

"Did he even notice Alex was back here?" Donovan marveled once the guy was gone, the scent of his spicy sub wafting in his wake.

"He deals with teenagers all day. I suspect it takes a lot to rile him."

"Maybe." Donovan bent and took the now-empty paper plate. "Guess Alex got his appetite back."

She dropped to her knee and rubbed the silky head. The puppy's gaze caught on hers, his brown eyes trusting as he stared up at her. "He sure is sweet."

"Don't let him fool you. He's a Lego thief."

Bellamy rubbed a bit harder before laughing when the puppy presented his belly for additional petting. "He's at risk of being spoiled." Pulling her hand back, she realized the potential danger of her lavish affection. "Should I be doing that? Am I going to put his training at risk?"

"There are hard-core guys among my numbers who may not agree with me, but I think part of his training is also knowing there's praise and affection. A few belly rubs after this evening's trauma shouldn't do too much damage."

When Alex's wiggles of ecstasy quickly faded to longer breaths and droopy eyes, she gave him a final pat and stood, coming face-to-face with Donovan.

Goodness, the man was attractive. His dark hair was cut close and showed off a sharply angled face and strong jaw. He was thick in build, but there wasn't an ounce of fat on him. Instead, he looked competent.

Capable.

And no one to mess with.

It made the warm eyes and sexy smile that much more powerful. Like she'd tempted him just the slightest bit to go against character.

"You mentioned closing out a busy year to that guy. You don't work here?"

"This is my parents' store. I grew up working here and can still be counted on to take a shift every now and again."

"This place is a Whisperwood institution."

She laughed at that, the description not quite how she'd have classified a small town corner store. "One they know about all the way up in Austin?"

"My family's here in Whisperwood. I grew up here and Mr. Reeves could always be counted on for a summer popsicle or a late night cup of coffee. I just came down for the evening for a family Christmas party and to put my dog at risk of my niece and her Legos."

She glanced at the clock and thought that eight was awfully early for an evening family party to end, but held the thought. Maybe they started early or maybe the kids had to go to bed. But…it raised questions.

"How long have you been a part of the APD?"

"I went in straight out of college, so a few years now. I've wanted K-9, and Alex is my first opportunity."

She did the quick math, estimating he was about four or five years younger than her. The thought was briefly unsettling—she usually went for older guys—but there was something about him that made the question of age seem more arbitrary than anything else.

Perhaps you've been looking in the wrong places, Bellamy Reeves.

Catching herself staring, she refocused on Alex. "You're responsible for his training?"

"A good part of it. There's a formal program for the entire K-9 team and their handlers, but we're paired. He lives with me and works with me."

She glanced down at the now-sleeping puppy and considered what that must be like. Fun, in a way, but what a responsibility. "What will he be able to do?"

"Once he's fully trained? He'll run the gamut on what he can find, including humans, drugs and bombs."

"Wow."

As she eyed the jean-clad form that even now leaned against her counter, she had to admit Donovan Colton made an impressive figure. And it wasn't just his body, though she could hardly deny that she found him attractive.

Wow was right.

There was an intensity about him. Some indefinable quality that intrigued her.

He was *interesting.* And she'd often found the opposite of attractive men, especially if her sister's long list of past boyfriends was any indication. It was as if somehow masculine features, a firm jaw and a sparkling smile negated any sense of humanity or interest in the world around them.

But not this guy.

"The K-9 team is designed to work across cases so we can go where we're needed. There are six others in the APD. Alex and I will make seven."

"It's impressive. And while he's obviously got great

promise, you've got a big year ahead of you. I wish you the best."

"Thanks." Donovan's gaze dropped toward the sleeping puppy before lifting back to her. "So if you don't work here, what do you do?"

"I'm an employee at Lone Star Pharmaceutical. I'm just helping out here since my parents had plans tonight."

"LSP. That's impressive. Are you a chemist or something?"

"No, I'm in finance." Ignoring the whisper through her mind of Maggie's continued admonitions to showcase herself in the best light, Bellamy pressed on. "They're wise to keep me away from beakers. Other than warming things up in a microwave, I avoid anything that involves cooking or open flames."

"Maybe I should consider inviting you to dinner, then, instead of risking you making anything behind that counter for me."

"Maybe."

"What time do you get off tonight?"

"I close up at ten and this is small town Texas. Nothing's open then."

"What about next week?"

"Sure. I—" She broke off when a distracted air came over his face, his hand dropping to the phone clipped at the waist of his jeans.

"I'm sorry. I'm getting a dispatch."

He excused himself and moved around the counter toward the door, his gaze morphing from friendly and sexy to straight cop.

Alex stirred, his senses on immediate alert at the emotional change in the atmosphere. He was on his feet and scrambling toward Donovan in a heartbeat. When he reached Donovan, he sat immediately, his little body arrow straight.

Bellamy marveled at it, the ease and trust she could already see between the two of them. If the dog was this responsive to training at ten weeks, she couldn't imagine what he'd become once fully grown.

The low tenor of Donovan's voice pulled her from her thoughts. Something had happened. Something bad, if his clipped responses were any indication.

"I'm sorry. I have to go. Can we take a rain check on that dinner?"

"Of course."

The sexy cop and his trusty sidekick were out of the store as fast as they came in and for several moments, Bellamy simply stood and watched the door where they'd disappeared, wondering if the evening had actually happened.

It was only when she got the call a half hour later that she knew the exact accident Donovan Colton was called to. And that the people he'd helped pull from two tons of wreckage were her parents.

Chapter One

The last strains of "Jingle Bells" faded out, giving way to "All I Want for Christmas Is You" as Bellamy Reeves clicked the last email in her inbox. Despite the multicolored lights she'd hung in her office and the music she'd determinedly turned on each morning and kept on low throughout the day, nothing seemed to get her in the holiday spirit.

Losing both parents over the summer had left a hole in her life and in her heart. She'd braced herself, of course, well aware the holidays would be a challenge. But even with the knowledge the season wouldn't be the same, she'd diligently clung to the belief she could find some sense of joy, somewhere.

How wrong she'd been.

The days seemed to drag, no matter how busy she made herself, and her job at Lone Star Pharmaceutical—a job she'd worked hard at for several years—couldn't fill the gaps.

"One more email," she whispered to herself on a resigned sigh. "I'll do the last one and cut out early."

The company was estimated to finish out the year with stellar earnings, and management had given everyone an extra day of comp time as a reward for all the hard work. Most people had used the time to go shopping for presents in nearby Austin or to take in the pretty decorations scattered throughout downtown Whisperwood. She'd done none of those things, not up for walking the sidewalks and making small talk with her fellow townsfolk.

Which had also meant she was still sitting on the extra time. Perhaps an afternoon off would provide a chance to recharge and shake the malaise that seemed determined to hover around her shoulders.

She missed her parents terribly, but it was also the first holiday in more than she could remember that wasn't encumbered by illness. Her father's loss of mobility five years before had taken a toll on all of them and her life had been filled with pill bottles, a wheelchair and ramps throughout the house, and bouts of belligerence that telegraphed DJ Reeves's frustration with his body's betrayal.

It hardly spoke well of her, that she was relieved that stage of life had passed, but in her quiet moments of honest reflection she could admit it was true.

Illness. Suffering. And an endless sort of wasting away that stole the joy out of life. All of it had affected her mother as surely as her father's loss of mobility in the accident had decimated his. Where her mother had once found joy in simple pleasures—gardening or cooking or even a glass of wine—watching her husband deteriorate had caused a matched response. Ginny Reeves had wasted away as surely as her husband had and nothing Bellamy had tried could coax her out of it.

The kidney failure that finally stole him from them in June had been the final straw for her mother. Her mental health had deteriorated rapidly after that, and the heart attack that took her in late July had almost seemed unavoidable.

"And here I am, right back to maudlin and depressed," she whispered to herself as she reached for the bottle of water she kept perpetually refilled on her desk.

The water had been another nod to health, her recognition of mortality—a fact of life with her parents, and an equally relevant fact of life working for a pharmaceutical company. Lone Star Pharmaceutical had hired her out of college and she'd steadily worked her way up through the ranks, responsible for any number of financial projects. For the past two years, she'd been part of the team that managed the costs to bring new drugs to market and had honed her skills around price elasticity, working with insurance companies and ensuring LSP had a place on doctors' prescription lists.

The role had been meant for her, honing her accounting knowledge and expanding her contribution to the overall business and its bottom line. She'd loved LSP already, but coupled with the professional advancement, her employer had also been understanding of her family situation. They'd allowed for flexible scheduling when she'd needed it and hadn't asked her to curtail the care and attention her parents needed.

She'd met enough people in waiting rooms at the hospital to know that flexibility was a gift beyond measure. The fact she'd also had an opportunity to still be considered for and receive promotions had cemented her sense of loyalty to LSP that was impossible to shake.

The company was a good one, with a focus on making life better for its consumers, its employees and even the community where it made its home—Whisperwood, Texas. Their CEO, Sutton Taylor, was a longtime resident and had stated on many occasions how important it was to him that his company have the same deep roots as he did.

Deep Texas *roots*, he usually clarified with a wink and a smile.

She couldn't hold back a faint smile of her own at the image of Sutton Taylor, standing tall in his suit and cowboy boots, proudly telling the employees how strong their year-end numbers looked. It wouldn't bring her parents back, but she could at least take some small joy in knowing she'd worked hard and contributed to a job well-done.

Satisfied she might leave the office on a glimmer of a bright note, Bellamy returned to her email, determined to tackle the last one before leaving for the afternoon.

The missive still bold because it was unread, Bellamy scanned the subject line, registering the odd description. RE: Vaccine Normalization.

Normalization of what?

The sender said INTERNAL, a company address she didn't immediately recognize, but she clicked anyway. A quick scan of the header information didn't show a named sender, either, nor was there anyone in the "To" list. Intrigued, Bellamy leaned forward, searching for anything that resembled usable details to describe what she was looking at.

Was it a virus?

That subject never failed to make her smile, the fact they had a department that battled real viruses housed in the same location as one who battled the digital kind.

The humor quickly gave way to the sobering details that filled the content of the note.

Bellamy caught the subject in snatches, the words practically blurring as she processed the odd, bulleted sentences.

LSP's virus vaccine, AntiFlu, will be distributed in limited quantities, with release schedule held in the strictest confidence.

Quantities are throttled to highest bidder, with market pricing increased to match quantity scarcity.

Management of egg supply has been secured.

If those points weren't bad enough, the closing lines of the email left no question as to what she was reading.

Lone Star Pharma has a zero-tolerance policy for discounted distribution of AntiFlu for the annual flu season. There will be no acceptance of annual contract prices with existing accounts.

Bellamy reread the email once, then again, the various details spiking her thoughts in different directions.

Throttled availability? Controlled pricing? Fixed scarcity?

And the fact there was mention of the egg supply—the incubation engine for production of the vaccine—was shocking.

What was this?

She read the note once more before scrolling back up to review the header details. The sender was veiled, but it did originate from an LSP email address.

Who would send this to her? And worse, why would

anyone possibly want to keep the very product they created for the public's good out of that same public's hands? She knew for a fact they had more than enough flu vaccine for the season. She also knew the scientific team had followed the CDC's guidelines for which strains of flu needed to be included.

She scrolled through the details once more, daring the words to change and prove her interpretation incorrect. But one more reread, or one hundred more, wasn't going to change the information housed in the email.

If this email was to be believed, the company she loved and believed in had turned to some dark and illegal practices.

"WELCOME BACK TO WHISPERWOOD, Alex. Quintessential small town Texas, from the tippy top of the big white gazebo smack in the middle of the town square, to the string of shops on Main Street."

Donovan Colton glanced over at his companion as he passed the gazebo and turned from Maple onto Main, unsurprised when he didn't receive a pithy response or even acknowledgment of his comment. As a matter of course, he'd have been more concerned if he *had* received a response.

His large black Lab possessed many talents, but a speaking voice wasn't one of them.

What Alex—short for Alexander the Great—did have was a nose that could sniff out explosive materials and he knew exactly how to translate that knowledge back to Donovan so he could in turn secure help. The fact Alex had several hundred million scent receptors in his nose—and had been trained almost since birth to use them in support of police work—meant Donovan had a powerful partner in their work to capture the bad guys.

It also helped he got along far better with his canine partner than he ever would have with a real live human one.

Donovan had been an animal lover since he was small. His various chores around the Colton ranch never seemed like chores if an animal was involved. Whether it was horse duty, mucking stalls or collecting eggs from the coops, he hadn't cared or seen any of it as work, so long as he got to spend time with the furry and the feathered Coltons who shared space on the large ranch that sprawled at the far west end of Whisperwood.

That love ran ever deeper to any number of mutts who had called the Colton ranch home.

Just like me, Donovan added to himself, the thought a familiar one.

Shaking it off, he focused on the gorgeous dog next to him. Donovan had loved each and every canine that had graced his life, but Alex was something extra special. Alex had been trained since puppyhood for life on a K-9 team; the two of them had bonded quickly, one an extension of the other. Alex looked to him for security, order, discipline and the clear role as alpha of their pack. In return, Donovan stroked, praised, and directed the animal into any number of search and rescue situations, confident his companion could handle the work.

And Alex always did.

From bombs to missing persons, Alex did his job with dedication, focus and—more often than not—a rapid wag of his tail.

Yep. Donovan would take a four-footed partner over one with two feet any day.

Not that he could technically complain about any of the fine men and women he'd worked with in the past, but something just *fit* with Alex. They had a bond and a way of working that was far easier than talking to someone.

Their trip to Whisperwood had been unusually quiet, he and Alex dispatched to an old warehouse site to confirm the Austin PD hadn't missed any drugs on a raid the prior week. The cache they had discovered had been worth millions and Donovan's captain wanted to ensure they hadn't overlooked anything.

Donovan's thorough site review hadn't revealed any missed stashes but it was Alex's attention to the crime scene that reinforced the fact the initial discovery team had found all there was to find. Donovan would bet his badge on it.

If Alex couldn't find it, it's because it didn't exist.

What it also meant was that his trip to Whisperwood was over far earlier than Donovan had planned.

And disappearing back out of town—especially after greeting the local chief of police at the crime scene—wasn't going to go down very well. If his mother knew he'd come through and hadn't stopped by, no amount of excuses could save him.

"You're just too damn good, Alex."

The dog's tongue lolled happily to the side while he maintained a steady view of the passing scenery outside the car. The use of his name had Alex's ears perking but even the warm tone couldn't distract the dog from the holiday wreaths hanging neatly from each lamppost in town.

Donovan took in the view, his memories of his hometown not too far off the mark of the real thing. The wreaths came out like clockwork the Monday before Thanksgiving, hanging until precisely the third day after the new year. A town committee changed out the ribbons on each wreath every week so they remained perfectly tied throughout the holiday. Red, green and gold, they alternated in a steady pattern, accompanied by bright, vibrant banners that wished people the happiness of the season.

His gaze drifted toward the corner store, an old memory pushing against his thoughts. A night, several Christmases past, when he'd had a sick little puppy and had flirted with a woman.

She'd been kind, he remembered, and pretty in a way that wasn't flashy, but that intrigued all the same. There was something solid there. Lasting, even. Which was silly, since he hadn't spent more than a half hour in her company before heading out on a call.

He'd thought to go in and ask about her a few times since, but training Alex had provided Donovan with a good excuse to stay out of his hometown; by the time he came back a year and a half later it had seemed lame—and far too late—to stop back in and ask about her.

But he did think of her every now and again. The slender form that filled out a pair of jeans with curves that had made his fingers itch and just enough skin showing at the top of her blouse to shift his thoughts in interesting, heated directions.

Dismissing the vague memory of pretty gray eyes and long, dark hair, he refocused on the pristine streets before him and the large ranch housed at the edge of town.

He needed to go see his mother. If he was lucky, his father would be out for the afternoon and he could avoid the lecture about coming to visit more often. He found it odd—funny, even—that it was his father who was more determined to deliver that particular guilt trip than his mother.

At the edge of the town square, Donovan looked at the large gazebo that dominated the space before putting on his blinker to head toward the Colton ranch. "Pretty as a picture."

At his comment, Alex's ears perked again and he turned from the view out the passenger window, his head tilted slightly toward Donovan.

"You don't miss a trick, do you?"

Donovan took his role as alpha in their relationship seriously, and that meant avoiding tension, anger or panic when speaking and working with Alex. Donovan had always innately understood an animal's poor acceptance of those emotions, but his K-9 training had reinforced it. He needed to stay calm and firm in the face of his furry partner, never allowing random, spiking emotions a place in their partnership.

Which meant the emotions that had the deepest of roots—established in the very foundation of his childhood—needed to be avoided at all costs. Especially if the prospect of visiting the Colton ranch was transmitted by his tone.

Extending a hand, he ruffled Alex's head and ears, scratching the spot he knew was particularly sensitive. A low, happy groan echoed from his partner when Donovan kneaded the small area behind Alex's ears, effectively erasing whatever tension he'd pushed into his police-issued SUV.

And on a resigned sigh, he made the turn that would carry him to the large ranch that sprawled for over a thousand acres deep in the heart of Texas Hill Country.

Home.

BELLAMY FOUGHT THE steady swirl of nerves that coated her stomach, bumping and diving like waves roiling on a winter's day as she walked the long corridor toward the human resources department. Lone Star Pharmaceutical had a sprawling campus and HR was three buildings away from her own, connected through a series of parking lots as well as overhead walkways for when the weather was poor or just too darn hot during a Texas summer.

She'd thought to call ahead and share her concerns but for reasons she couldn't quite explain to herself, ultimately decided on a surprise approach.

Was she even supposed to have the email?

The sender was veiled, but so was the distribution list. She didn't even know why she'd been targeted for such information.

Snatches of the email floated through her mind's eye, each destructive word adding another pitch and roll to those waves.

Limited quantities...throttled to highest bidder... quantity scarcity...

No acceptance of annual contract prices.

Was this the reason for the exceptionally strong year at LSP? Were they all celebrating extra time off and assured holiday bonuses at the expense of human lives?

She'd worked in finance her entire life and monitoring the ebbs and flows of the business was a part of her day to day. She understood balance sheets and marketplace pricing. She understood profit and loss statements. And she understood what it took to run an ethical business that still remained profitable.

And creating a scarcity in the market—*deliberately*—was not legal.

But it could be very, very profitable.

All the drugs LSP produced were essential for the individuals who needed them. They led the market on several fronts, with specialties in diabetes, heart disease and cholesterol reducing medicines. LSP had also done wonders with drugs designed to improve motor skills, several of which had been essential to her father's well-being.

But the flu vaccine was a whole different issue.

For anyone suffering from an illness, access to proper care and medicine was essential, but the flu affected everyone. A bad season could kill a large number of people, especially those at highest risk.

Just like her parents.

Had her father forgone a flu vaccine for the last several years of his life, he'd surely have been at higher risk of dying from the virus. And the fewer people vaccinated, the higher the risk.

Was it really possible LSP was attempting to profit from that?

Technically, they were late in the season to get the vaccine, but even as late as the prior week she'd run the numbers and realized that immunizations were down versus the prior year.

Was that because too many people felt they didn't need protection?

Or because there wasn't any protection in the market?

She tamped down on another wave of bile cresting in her stomach and knocked on the open door of the HR department. She'd been at LSP long enough to know several members of the HR team but wasn't acquainted with the head of HR, Sally Borne.

A light "come in" echoed through the cavernous outer office. Bellamy understood why the voice sounded so far away when she saw only one person seated in what appeared to be a sea of about six desks. She headed for the woman, taking in the office along the way. Decorations celebrating the holiday season peppered the walls and filing cabinets, and a bright string of lights hung from the ceiling over a table that held a pretty menorah as well as a beautifully carved wooden kinara holding the seven candles of Kwanzaa.

This holiday sentiment was matched throughout the five buildings of LSP and reflected Sutton Taylor's stated goals of inclusion and celebration of diversity. It had been yet one more facet of life at LSP and one more reason she loved where she worked.

Could someone who believed so deeply in humanity and culture and individuality be so soulless as to withhold essential drugs for the good of others?

"Can I help you?" The lone woman smiled, her voice kind as she stood behind her desk, effectively welcoming Bellamy in.

"I'd like to speak to Sally Borne."

"What's this regarding?"

"It's a private matter."

There was the briefest flash of awareness in the woman's bright blue eyes before she nodded. "Let me see if Sally has a few minutes in her schedule. I'll be right back."

Pleasant smile for a watchdog, Bellamy thought.

The idea struck swiftly and was at odds with the sense of inclusion that had welcomed her into the human resources department.

The woman disappeared toward a wall of frosted windows that allowed in light but made it impossible to see through. The windows covered what appeared to be one large office that extended across the back of the space. While it was to be expected—Human Resources dealt with any number of private matters—something about the glass made her think of a prison.

Which only reinforced just how far gone her thoughts had traveled since reading the email.

This was Human Resources, for Pete's sake. The department in all of Lone Star Pharmaceutical that was designed to help the employees.

Bellamy had worked with HR during her flex time requests when she was caring for her parents and they'd been kind and deeply understanding. They'd been in a different building then, only recently having moved into this space in the main building that housed the LSP executive staff.

Sally Borne was new to the company, as well. She'd replaced their retiring HR lead in the fall and had already implemented several new hiring initiatives as well as a new employee training program that was rolling out department by department. The woman was a leader and, by all accounts, good for Lone Star Pharmaceutical. Painting her as some fire-breathing dragon behind a retaining wall wasn't going to get Bellamy anywhere.

Especially as those waves in her stomach continued to roil, harder and harder, as she waited for the meeting.

The sensation was so at odds with her normal experience at work. She'd become accustomed to the frustration and fear that came from managing her father's care, but LSP had always been a safe haven. She loved her job and her work and found solace in the routine and the sense of accomplishment. At LSP, she was in control.

So why did she feel so *out* of control since opening that damn email?

"Are you ready?" The lone HR worker reappeared from Sally's office, her smile still firmly intact.

"Thank you."

Bellamy ignored the sense of being watched, and headed for the inner domain, hidden along the back wall. There was neither a fire-breathing dragon nor anything to worry about. *She*'d been sent the suspicious email. Coming to HR was simply about doing her job.

More, it was about being responsible to it.

"Hello." Sally Borne met her at the door, her hand extended and that same bright smile highlighting her face. "I'm Sally."

Bellamy introduced herself, then provided a sense of her role in the company. "I'm part of the financial team that manages the process of bringing new drugs to market."

"Andrew Lucas's team?"

"Yes, Andrew is my boss."

Sally nodded and pursed her lips before extending a hand toward her desk. Bellamy followed her, settling herself in a hard visitor's chair while Sally took her position behind a large oak monstrosity that looked like it belonged in Sutton Taylor's office.

Sally scribbled something on a blank legal pad, her attention focused on the paper. "Is Andrew aware you're here?"

Bellamy forced a small smile, unwilling to have the woman think she was here to complain about her boss. "Andrew's not the reason I'm here."

"But does he know you're here?"

"No."

"How can I help you then, Ms. Reeves?"

The prospect of sharing the details of what she'd discovered had haunted Bellamy throughout the walk from her office to HR, but now that she was here, the reality of what she had to share became stifling. Whether she'd been the intended recipient or not, the information she held was damning in the extreme. Anyone within LSP who would make such a decision or declaration would surely be fired. Worse, the possibility of jail time had to be a distinct consideration. They might be a for-profit company, but they still worked for the public good.

Was she really sure of what she'd come to discuss with HR?

Even as she asked herself the question, the memory of what she had read in the email steeled her resolve.

She was sitting on a problem and rationalizing it away at a personal moment of truth was unfair at best, flat out immoral at worst.

"I received an odd email today and I felt it was important to discuss it with you directly."

"Odd?" Sally's hands remained folded on top of her

desk but the vapid smile that had ridden her features faded slightly.

"There wasn't a named sender, for starters."

"We have effective spam filters on our email but things can slip through. Do you think that was it?"

"No, no, I don't. The email just said 'internal.'"

"And no one signed it?"

"No."

Something small yet insistent began to buzz at the base of Bellamy's spine. Unlike the concern and panic that had flooded her system upon realizing what the email held, this was a different sort of discomfort. Like how animals in the forest scented a fire long before it arrived.

A distinct sense of danger began to beat beneath her skin.

"Here. Look at this." Bellamy pulled the printout she'd made out of the folder she'd slipped it into, passing it across the desk. "If you look at the top, you can see it came from the LSP domain."

Sally stared at the note, reading through the contents. Her expression never changed, but neither did that vague sense of menace Bellamy couldn't shake. One that grew darker when Sally laid the paper on her desk, pushing it beneath her keyboard.

"This is a poor joke, Ms. Reeves."

"A joke?"

"You come in here and suggest someone's sending you inappropriate messaging, then you hand me a note that's something out of a paranoid fantasy. What sort of sabotage are you intending to perpetrate against LSP?"

"I'm trying to prevent it."

"By forging a note and tossing it around like you're some affronted party?"

Affronted party? Forgery? The damn thing had popped into *her* inbox a half hour ago.

"This was sent to me."

Even as Bellamy's temperature hit a slow boil, Sally Borne sat across from her as if she were the injured party. "Are you sure about that? It would be easy enough to make a few changes in a photo alteration program and muster this up. Or perhaps you're even more skilled and able to hack into our email servers."

"You can't be serious. I received this email. Pull up the server files yourself if you're so convinced they've been tampered with."

"I'm sure that won't be necessary."

Bellamy sat back, her ire subsiding in the face of an even more unbelievable truth. The director of Human Resources didn't believe her. "You do understand the implications of something like this?"

"I most certainly do."

Although this wasn't the same as losing her parents, Bellamy couldn't fully shake the sadness and, worse, the acute sense of loss at Sally Borne's callous disregard for her word. Her truth. With one last push, she tried to steer the conversation back to steady ground.

"Who could possibly be sending messages like this? What are they trying to accomplish? And who else might have received something like this?"

"You tell me." Sally waved an idle hand in the direction of the email now lodged beneath her keyboard. "You're the one in possession of the mysterious email. No one else has called me or sent me any others to review." Sally's gaze never wavered as she stared back from her side of the large desk, her words landing like shards of ice as they were volleyed across that imposing expanse.

"Which I'm trying to get your help with. Could you imagine if this were really true?" Bellamy asked, willing the woman to understand the gravity of the situation. "We'd be putting millions of lives at risk."

Only when Sally only stared at her, gaze determinedly blank, did the pieces begin to click into place.

"So it's true, then? LSP *is* tampering with vaccines." The words came out on a strangled whisper.

"What's true is that you're a financial leader at this company determined to spread lies and disruption," Sally snapped back.

"I'm not—"

A brisk knock at the door had Bellamy breaking off and turning to see the same woman from the outer office. "Ms. Borne. Here are the details you asked for."

A large file was passed over the desk and Bellamy saw her name emblazoned on the tab of the thick folder.

Her employment file?

"Thank you, Marie." Sally took the folder as the helpful, efficient Marie rushed back out of the office.

It was only when the file was laid down that Bellamy saw a note on top. The writing was neat and precise and easily visible across the desk.

10+ year employee.
Steadfast, determined, orderly.
Both parents died in past year.

She was under evaluation here? And what would her parents' deaths have to do with anything?

Sally tapped the top before opening the manila file. Thirteen years of performance reviews and salary documentation spilled from the edges, but it was that note on top that seemed to echo the truth of her circumstances.

For all her efforts to make a horrible situation right, something had gone terribly wrong.

"Is there a reason you felt the need to pull my personnel file?"

"A matter of routine."

"Oh? What sort of routine?"

"When an employee is behaving in a suspicious manner, I like to understand what I'm dealing with."

"Then you'll quickly understand you're dealing with a highly competent employee who has always received stellar reviews and professional accolades."

Sally flipped back to the cover, her gaze floating once more over the attached note. "I also see a woman who's suffered a terrible loss."

While she'd obviously registered the note about her parents when the file was dropped off, nothing managed to stick when she tried to understand where Sally was going with the information. "I lost my parents earlier this year."

"Both of them."

"Yes."

"Were they in an accident?"

"My father has been ill for many years, the repercussions of a serious accident. My mother's health, unfortunately, deteriorated along with his."

"It's sad." Sally traced the edge of the damn note again, the motion drawing attention to the seemingly random action. "Illness like that takes a toll."

A toll? *Obviously.* "Dying is a difficult thing. Nothing like the slow fading we see on TV."

Sally continued that slow trace of the paper. "It's also an expensive thing."

"You can't possibly think—"

"It's exactly what I think." The steady, even-keeled woman was nowhere in evidence as Sally stood to her full height, towering over her desk like an avenging cobra. "And you think it, too. You dare to come in here, convinced you can blackmail this company into giving you money for some concocted lie of immense proportions."

"You can't think that."

"I can and I do. And I want you to pack your office immediately. Security will escort you there and off the premises."

"But I—"

Sally pointedly ignored her, tapping on her phone to summon Marie. When the woman scrambled in, Sally didn't even need to speak. Marie beat her to it. "Security will be here momentarily."

"Excellent." Sally shifted her attention once more, her gaze fully trained on Bellamy as she pointed toward the door. "Don't expect a reference."

Dazed, Bellamy stood and moved toward the exit. The meeting had been nothing like what she'd expected. Surreal at best, even as she had to admit it was fast becoming a nightmare.

Lone Star Pharmaceutical had been her professional home for more than thirteen years and in a matter of moments, that home had been reduced to nothing more than rubble and ash.

Chapter Two

Donovan glanced around the large, welcoming, airy living room of the main Colton ranch house as his mother settled two glasses of iced tea on the coffee table. She'd already bustled in with a tray of his favorites—cheese and crackers, a bowl of cashews and a tray of gooey Rice Krispies Treats—and had topped it off with her world famous sweet tea.

Perhaps that was a stretch, but she had brought her tea to every gathering ever held in Whisperwood. Someone had even asked him about it at work one day, rumors of his mother's special recipe having reached as far as Austin. Donovan reached for his glass and took a sip, more than ready to admit every sugary drop deserved its near-reverent reputation.

"I'm so glad you're here." She glanced down at Alex, her smile indulgent as she pet his head. "Glad you're both here. Though to what do I owe the pleasure?"

"Alex and I had a job that finished early. I thought I'd come over and visit before heading back to Austin."

"I'm glad you did. Our last dinner ended too early. And I—" She broke off, shaking her head. "I'm glad you're here."

Memories of his last dinner with his family still

stuck in his gut and Donovan avoided thinking about it. He loved them—he always had—but he couldn't be who they wanted him to be. And he'd long past stopped trying. Their definition of family was different from his and he'd spent a lifetime trying to reconcile that fact.

And was coming up damn short, truth be told.

He reached for a handful of cashews and ignored the guilt that poked beneath his ribs with pointy fingers. He was here, wasn't he? That had to count for something.

Even if his presence was grudging at best.

"He's so good."

His mother's words pulled Donovan from his musings and he glanced over to where she'd settled Alex's head onto her lap, his gaze adoring as he stared up at her. "All this food and he hasn't even looked at it."

"Oh, he's looking. Don't let him fool you."

"But he's so good and doesn't even attempt to make a play for anything. Remember Bugsy. That dog could find food if you wrapped it in plastic and buried it in the back of the pantry. He'd find a way to get to it, too."

Unbidden, memories of the small, crafty mutt they'd had when Donovan was in high school filled his thoughts. Bugsy was a good dog—as friendly as he was tenacious—and his forays into the Colton pantry had become the stuff of family legend. "He didn't miss much."

"I always assumed all dogs were that way, but Alex is amazing. He hasn't moved an inch."

"He's a formally trained police dog. It wouldn't do to have him nosing into pockets at crime scenes or roaming through the pantry on home visits. He's trained to sniff out bomb materials and illegal drugs."

"Yes, he is. A dangerous job for a brave boy." Her attention remained on the dog but Donovan was acutely aware the comment was meant for him.

"When the bad guys stop being bad guys, he can slow down."

"I suppose so." His mother patted Alex's head. "But for the record, I am all for a dog being a dog. I did enjoy documenting some of Bugsy's escapades."

"There aren't many like him."

"Remember that Christmas he ate all the cookies? Oh boy, was that dog sick."

Donovan remembered that holiday—along with the mess the dog vomited up in the barn later that morning—but true to form Bugsy had been back in business in no time. The wily dog raided the bacon and black-eyed peas on New Year's Day, barely a week later.

"He was a character."

The shift to a safe topic put them back on neutral ground and they fell silent again, his mother's soft smile focused on Alex and the large black head snuggled in her lap. She might not be his biological mother, but Donovan had always known he'd gotten his love of animals from Josephine Colton. Her gentle nature and genuine pleasure with the furry or the feathered had always been a hallmark of her personality.

His mother had never met a stray she didn't love or an animal she couldn't whisper sweet nothings to. And since he'd been a stray himself, Donovan had innately understood the value in that personality trait.

"Dad keeping busy?"

"As much as the doctor allows. Your father is frustrated he can't do the things he used to."

"There's no shame in asking for help."

His mother sighed, trouble flashing in her warm brown eyes before she dropped her gaze back to Alex. "There is, apparently, when your name is Hays Colton."

"He comes by that one honestly, don't you think? In fact, I'd say he comes from a very long line of stubborn Coltons, starting with Uncle Joe and working his way down."

The words were enough to vanquish the spot of trouble in her eyes and she smiled at that. "For someone who claims they can't remember the names of so many aunts, uncles and cousins, you sure can pull them out readily enough when making a point."

"The beauty of a large family." *An adopted one*, Donovan added to himself. He'd managed to hold those words back this time. Coupled with the fact that he and his mother were having a cordial afternoon, Donovan figured he might actually get out of his childhood home without offending anyone or causing a fresh bout of tears.

Because, try as he might, there wasn't any amount of love or extended family or years-old shared stories that could change one fundamental fact: Josephine and Hays Colton weren't actually his parents.

And while Donovan would be eternally grateful for their care, their upbringing and their name, he'd never quite gotten past the circumstances that had put him in their barn one cold Christmas morning, abandoned and alone.

BELLAMY MARCHED THE return trip back to her office building from the human resources department. The walk had been long enough that she'd already worked her way through the first stage of grief—denial—and was fast barreling toward number two.

Anger.

How dare they? Or how dare *she*? Despite the reputation that had spread quickly about Sally Borne's competence since her arrival at LSP, Bellamy still couldn't get over the woman's gall. Nor could she see past the horrifying thought that Sally thought she was somehow responsible for that awful note.

"Are you okay, Ms. Reeves?"

She turned at the sweet voice of Gus Sanger, doing his level best to keep up with her long strides through the above-ground corridors that connected the buildings.

"I'm fine."

"I've known you a long time, young lady. You're not fine. And that was no simple visit to HR."

"It's a private matter."

"Meetings in HR usually are." Gus tugged at his ear, but kept pace next to her now that they'd slowed a bit. "I've known you since you were small. Your parents' store was a key stop for me every morning on my drive to LSP and more often than not, you'd find your way behind that counter, fixing me a coffee and a muffin. You're a good girl, Bellamy Reeves, and whatever that private matter was about, you don't deserve an escort off the grounds."

The tears that had prickled the backs of her eyes intermittently since leaving Sally's office spiked once more but she held them back. She'd cried enough tears for a lifetime the past six months and refused to shed the same emotion over a situation that she hadn't caused, nor was she responsible for.

"Thanks, Gus."

"I don't care what HR says about me watching you like a common criminal. You go back to your office and take a few minutes to pack up. I'll wait for you in the lobby. It'll give me a chance to get some coffee."

"But what if HR catches you? Won't you get in trouble?"

Gus waved a hand. "If HR has a problem with me, they're going to have to go through Sutton. He may have his moments, acting like a damn fool ladies' man, but he and I went fishing in Whisperwood Creek when we were both seven years old. Been fishing there off and on ever since together. No one's firing me."

Bellamy smiled at the image—the grizzled Gus and the erudite Sutton Taylor, casting lines off the side of the creek. The "ladies' man" comment was a bit bold, even for Gus, but Bellamy was hardly unaware of Taylor's reputation.

"You've known each other a long time."

"A lifetime. All it would take is a few words to him and we can fix this."

"No, Gus." She shook her head before gentling her tone at the sincere offer of help. "I can't tell you how much I appreciate it, but I need to take care of this myself."

"If you're sure?"

"I'm sure. I'll find a way to fix this. To fix it all."

Gus nodded before using his badge to open the door to Bellamy's building. "Okay, then. I'll get my coffee and wait here. You take your time."

"Thank you."

A large staircase rose out of the lobby toward the second floor and Bellamy started up the stairs toward her office, another one of her daily concessions to health and wellness. The hallways were even emptier than when she'd left for Human Resources—had it really only been an hour?—and she passed a few pockets of conversation and could hear one of her colleagues talking in muted tones from inside his office.

What would they tell Andrew?

She liked her boss. They'd worked well since she'd been put on his team two years prior and she'd like to tell him in person what was going on. Share her side of the story. But he'd already departed a few weeks early for the holidays, taking his family on a long-planned trip to Hawaii.

The fleeting thought of texting him faded as she imagined what she'd even try to say.

Sorry to bother you on vacation. I just got fired because we're tampering with the flu vaccine supply chain here at LSP.

No way.

Even if she did want to bother him, what would he do from four thousand miles away? What she needed to do was take stock and evaluate what had happened. Then she could decide the best course of action. She was a well-respected employee at LSP and a member of the community. She'd find a way through this.

Even if Sally's comments at the end had taken a toll. Bellamy's father's accident and subsequent financial troubles weren't exactly a secret. She'd even had to sell the family business—the long-standing corner store her father had opened in his twenties—to pay for his medical bills.

No matter how sympathetic or understanding people might have been, it wasn't a far leap to think they'd believe Sally's innuendo.

It's sad.

Illness like that takes a toll.

It's also an expensive thing.

Each miserable word had stamped itself in her mind and Bellamy was hard-pressed to see how she'd come out in the best light should Sally decide to spread those rumors.

On a resigned sigh, she reached for the box Gus had handed her before departing for his coffee. Thirteen years, and she was left with a brown box and the few items she could stow inside.

The photo of her parents out front of the store—one of her favorites—came off her credenza first, followed by her calendar, a silly glass elf she'd purchased a few years before and the small radio that was still playing Christmas songs. She added a personnel file she'd kept her records in, a handful of cards given from coworkers through the years and, last, a few copies of the email she'd printed for herself.

Although she suspected even the affable Gus would have to take back any files she attempted to remove from her desk, she did a quick sweep of her files to make sure she hadn't missed anything.

And saw the framed photo of her sister, Maggie, she'd shoved in the bottom drawer. A dazzling smile reflected back at her, the remembered warmth there stabbing into Bellamy's heart.

She missed her sister. Desperately. And far more

than she probably should, even as she blamed Maggie for all that had gone wrong over the past five years.

Her sister's abandonment had stung, but it was the cold shoulder Maggie had given her at their parents' funerals that had hurt the most. When had her bright, beautiful, vibrant sister become such a cold witch?

The urge to toss the photo into the garbage, along with a few of the folders that held out-of-date information or pamphlets on some of their older drug introductions, was strong, but in the end familial loyalty won out and she shoved the frame facedown on top of the small pile of items in her cardboard box. If she was going to toss the picture, she could do it properly at home, not in a snit in what was soon to be someone else's office.

Shaking off the personal reminder of her relationship with her sister, Bellamy finished placing the last few items in the box. The printouts of the email that had started it all were the last to go in and, on impulse, she took the printouts from the box and secured them in her purse. "At least I have something."

The copy wasn't much but it did have a time and date stamp on it, and if she were able to secure a legal representative who could subpoena the company's electronic records, she might be able to prove the fact the email had been sent to her and was not a result of her own tampering.

With a hard tug on the closure of her purse, Bellamy stopped herself and fell into her chair.

Subpoena? Electronic records? Legal representation?

How had she gone from a fiercely loyal employee

to someone ready to instigate legal action in a matter of minutes?

The vibration of her phone caught her moments before the ringer went off, her best friend Rae's name and picture filling the screen. She toyed with not answering when the overwhelming urge to talk to someone who believed her struck hard.

"Hey there."

"What's wrong? You sound upset."

Bellamy smiled despite the horrible weight that had pressed on her chest since leaving Sally Borne's office. The quick response after a simple greeting was straight-up Rae and at that moment, Bellamy couldn't have been more grateful.

"Well. Um." The tears that had threatened on the walk back tightened her throat once more. "I'm packing my office."

"What? Why?" The noise of the Whisperwood General Store echoed in the background, but nothing in the noise could dim Rae's concern. "Who would do that? You're one of their best employees."

"As of a half hour ago, they began treating me like Enemy Number One."

"What? Wait—" Rae broke off, the din in the background fading even as she hollered at someone to come help her at the counter. "Okay. I'm in my office. Talk to me."

Bellamy laid it all out—the email, the walk to HR and the weird meeting, even Gus's kindness in letting her have a few minutes.

"Gus'll give Sutton Taylor what for. Why don't you let him?"

"I need to process this. Something's going on and

the faster I figure out what it is, the faster I can get my job back." *If I even want it.*

The thought was so foreign—and such a departure from who she'd been for the past thirteen years—Bellamy nearly repeated the words out loud.

Was it possible the damage of an afternoon could remove the goodwill of nearly a decade and a half?

"Who do you think did it?" Rae's question interrupted the wending of Bellamy's thoughts.

"I wish I knew. It's dangerous, Rae. If it's a joke it's a horrific slander on the company. And if it's true—" Bellamy stopped, barely able to finish the thought. "If it's true, it's a problem beyond measure. We serve the public good. We can't take that good away from them, especially in flu season."

"I've already had a few people in complaining about it. I'm tempted to drag on a surgical mask each morning before I open up."

Rae would do it, too, Bellamy thought with a smile. That and a whole lot more, she had to admit.

"Look, Rae. I need you to keep this to yourself until I understand what's going on."

"Bell, come on, you have to tell someone."

"I will. But. Well. Look, just don't say anything, okay? Please promise me."

The quiet was nearly deafening before she heard her friend acquiesce through the phone. "Okay. I'll hold my tongue for now."

"Thank you. Let me get my feet under me and I can figure out what comes next."

"So long as it entails a visit to the police at some point."

Since her thoughts hadn't been too far from the

same, Bellamy had to admit Rae had a point. "I'll call you later. I need to finish packing up and get out of here. Even with Gus's willingness to give me time, the dragon in HR is going to expect me off the grounds."

"Okay. Call me later."

They hung up with a promise to do a good raging girls' night, complete with margaritas and a gallon of ice cream. It couldn't erase her day, but as promises went it was certainly something to look forward to.

Bellamy glanced down at her box, her meager possessions all she had as evidence of her time at Lone Star Pharmaceutical.

Securing the lid, she took a deep breath and pulled her purse over her arm.

She'd already lived through the loss of her family, both through death and through abandonment. She would survive this.

Resolved, Bellamy picked up the box and walked out of her office. She refused to look back.

THE MID-DECEMBER AFTERNOON light was fading as Bellamy trudged toward her car. She'd snagged a spot in the far back parking lot, beneath an old willow that she loved for its sun protection and the added benefit of more daily steps, to and from the front door. Now it just seemed like more punishment as she put one foot in front of the other, her box completing the professional walk of shame.

Thankfully, the parking lot was rather empty, the impending holiday and the general spirit of celebration and success at LSP pushing even more people than she'd expected to knock off early.

Gus had been kind when he met her in the lobby,

his expression sorrowful as he took her badge and her corporate credit card. Sally Borne hadn't shown up for the proceedings but her office lackey, Marie, had been there to take the badge and credit card before bustling off back where she'd come from.

It was unkind, but Bellamy hadn't been able to dismiss the image of a small crab scuttling back to its sandy burrow the way the woman rushed off.

And then it had just been awkward with Gus, so she'd given him a quick kiss on the cheek and a warm hug, promising to visit with him in town at the annual tree lighting in the town square the following week. She'd already committed to Rae that she'd go and she'd be damned if she was going to hide in her home like the same crab she'd mentally accused Marie of being.

Shifting the box in her arms, Bellamy laid it on her rear bumper as she dug for her keys. After unlocking the car, then pressing the button for her trunk, she juggled the box into the gaping maw of her sedan, only to fumble it as she attempted to settle it with one hand while her other held her purse in place.

A steady stream of expletives fell from her lips when a brisk wind whipped up, catching the now-loose box lid and flinging it from the trunk.

"Damn it!"

The temptation to leave the lid to fly from one end of the parking lot to the other was great, but she dutifully trudged off to snag it where it drifted over the concrete. She might be persona non grata but she wouldn't add litterbug to the litany of sudden crimes she'd apparently perpetrated against LSP. Nor would she put someone at risk of tripping on it inadvertently.

Box lid in hand, she crossed back to the car, dropping into the driver's seat and turning on the ignition. The car caught for the briefest moment, then rumbled to life. She put her foot on the brake, about to shift into reverse, when her gaze caught on the rearview mirror and her still-open trunk.

Resigned, she opened the door once more and crossed back to the trunk. That damn cardboard box stared up at her, the lonely receptacle of her professional life and—finally—she let the tears she'd fought all afternoon fall.

Lost job. Lost family. Hell, even a holiday that was shaping up to be a lost cause. All of it seemed to conspire against her until all she could see or think or feel was an overwhelming sense of loss.

Frustrated, Bellamy stepped back and slammed the lid.

Instantly, a wall of heat flared up, consuming her before she felt her body lifted off the ground and thrown across the parking lot.

DONOVAN WAS MIDWAY down his parents' stone-covered driveway when the call from Dispatch came in. He answered immediately, responding with his badge number and his location.

"We have a bomb called in at Lone Star Pharmaceutical. Your location indicates you're closest to the site."

LSP?

An image of the imposing corporate park on the edge of Whisperwood filled his thoughts, along with the pretty woman he'd met a million years ago who worked there. Who was bombing the town's largest employer? And why?

"I am," Donovan confirmed. "I can be to the site in three minutes. What are the known details?"

"LSP security called it in. Initial report says a car on fire and a woman shaky but standing."

"She walked away from a car bomb?"

"Reports say she was outside it and tossed back by the blast."

"I'm on my way."

"Thanks, Officer. Backup will meet you there."

Donovan took a left out of his parents' driveway instead of the right he'd planned. Flipping on his lights he headed out over the two-lane Farm to Market road that lead back into town and on toward the corporate headquarters that stood at the opposite edge of Whisperwood.

He'd already spent the morning with the town's chief of police and now it looked like he'd spend his evening with him, as well. The town was big enough to keep a sizable force, but they had to tap into the Austin PD for specialties like bomb squad support. As LSP had grown along with the town, Donovan had often wondered why the local PD hadn't been given more resources, but knew that wasn't always an easy battle.

It was one that big companies readily fought when they preferred to employ their own security.

Perhaps that folly had come back to bite them?

By all accounts LSP's owner was a local maverick who was as delighted to be a pillar of the community as he was to rub the town's noses in it when he wanted to do things his way. Bold and daring, Sutton Taylor had favored the town he'd grown up in to set up his world-renowned pharmaceutical company.

Donovan turned onto Lone Star Boulevard, the well-paved road that ran in front of LSP's headquarters. The scrub grass and occasional ruts that made up the drive across town vanished as he came onto LSP land.

The guards at the main entrance waved him through the gates before he'd barely flashed his badge and Donovan headed straight for the billowing smoke still evident at the back of the parking lot. Alex sat sentinel beside him, his body strung tight as a bow as he waited for his orders.

Even from a distance, Donovan could tell the scene was contained. Two LSP security vehicles were parked near the still-smoldering car and a crowd had gathered at the edge of the parking lot, obviously evacuated from the building. The security team seemed to have it under control, the individuals corralled far enough back to avoid any additional fallout from the wrecked car. With the destruction already wrought on the burning sedan, the car was the least likely source of any remaining danger.

Instead, he and Alex would go to work on the scattered vehicles still in the lot.

He parked, his already alert partner rising farther up on his seat. Within a few moments, he had Alex at his side, leashed and ready for duty. One of the security guards moved away from a huddled woman and walked toward him. The man was grizzled, his body stiff with age, but his clear blue eyes were bright and alert.

Sharp.

The man nodded. "Officer. I'm Gus Sanger. I'm in Security here at LSP."

"Donovan Colton. This is Alex." He motioned for Alex to sit beside him, the move designed to show his control over the animal yet ensure no one missed the dog's imposing presence.

"You got here fast. K-9's out of the Austin PD."

"I was in Whisperwood on another assignment." Donovan shook the proffered hand before pointing toward a pretty woman covered in soot. "Is she hurt?"

"Claims she isn't. That's Ms. Reeves. Bellamy Reeves. She's banged up and has a few scratches on her elbows and a bigger gash on her arm the EMTs bandaged up, but I'd say lucky all in all."

At the utterance of her name, Donovan stilled. Although he hoped it didn't show to Sanger, Alex recognized it immediately, shifting against his side.

Bellamy Reeves? The same woman he'd spoken to so many years ago in the Whisperwood corner store…

"Do you mind if I go talk to her?"

Sanger nodded, his gaze dropping to Alex. "Does he go everywhere with you?"

"Everywhere."

"Good."

Donovan walked to the woman, taking her in as he went. She was turned, her gaze focused on her car, but he could make out her profile and basic build. Same long legs. Same sweep of dark hair. And when she finally turned, he saw those same alert gray eyes, that were mysterious and generous, all at the same time.

She was still pretty, even beneath a layer of dirt and grime from whatever happened to her car. Which he'd get to in a moment. First, he wanted to see her.

"Ms. Reeves?"

She had her arms crossed, the bandage Gus mentioned evident on her forearm and her hands cradled against her ribs as if hugging herself. She was drawn in—scared, by his estimation—and doing her level best to hide it. "Officer?"

He ordered Alex to heel at his side, then extended his hand. "I'm Officer Colton. This is Alex. We're here to help you."

Whether it was the use of their names or the fading shock of the moment, her eyes widened. "You."

"It's me. How are you, Bellamy?"

Those pretty eyes widened, then dropped to Alex. "He's so big. Just like I knew he would be." She instinctively reached for Alex before pulling her hand back.

"You can pet him if you'd like. He's not formally working yet."

She bent, her gaze on Alex as her hands went to cup the Lab's head and ears. Donovan didn't miss how they trembled or what a calming effect Alex seemed to have on her as she petted that soft expanse of fur. "You grew just as big as I knew you would. But I hope you've learned some restraint around plastic toys."

"Grudgingly." Donovan smiled when she glanced back up at him, pleased that she'd remembered them. "We nearly had a repeat incident with a few Barbie high heels but I managed to recover them before he swallowed them."

"He's a little thief."

"One who fortunately matured out of the impulse."

She stood back upright but kept a slightly less shaky hand on Alex's head. "You're here because of this?"

"I was in town on another assignment today and hadn't left yet. Are you okay?" The assignment was a bit of a stretch but somehow, saying he had to visit his mother or risk her wrath didn't seem like the most comforting comment.

"I'm fine. Gus looked at me quickly and I don't feel hurt other than the scrapes. Shaken and sort of wobbly, but nothing hurts too bad or feels broken."

"How close were you to the car?"

"I'd gotten in and realized I hadn't closed the trunk. I was behind the car when it just—" She broke off, the disbelief still clear in her eyes. "When it just exploded."

"We're going to take a look at it but first I need Alex to sniff the rest of the cars that are still here so we can get these people out of here. Can you wait for me?"

"Where else am I going to go?"

For reasons Donovan couldn't explain, he sensed there was something more in her comment. Something that went well beyond a car bomb or the shaky aftereffects of surviving a crime.

Something terrible had taken the light out of her beautiful gray eyes.

And he was determined to find out why.

Chapter Three

Bellamy stood to the side and watched the chaos that had overtaken the parking lot. Several cop cars had arrived shortly after Donovan and Alex as well as two fire trucks and the EMTs. At one point she'd estimated half of Whisperwood's law enforcement had found its way to LSP. The scene was well controlled and she'd been happy to see how the local police handled the press who were already sniffing around for a story. They were currently corralled on the far edge of the property, clamoring for whatever scraps they could get.

She'd ignored them, even as one had somehow secured her cell phone number and had already dialed her three times. It was probably only the start and she'd finally turned off the ringer. There would be time enough to deal with the fallout once she knew what she was actually dealing with.

And it might be to her advantage to have a working relationship with someone from the press if she needed to tell her side of the story.

If? Or when? a small voice inside prompted.

Sighing, she let her gaze wander back over the assembled crowd of law enforcement. Would they help her if she truly needed it? Or would they bow to whatever pressure LSP might put on them?

Like a bucket of errant Ping-Pong balls, the thoughts winged around in her mind, volleying for position and prominence.

She'd already taken the proffered water and over-the-counter pain meds from the EMT attendant and had finally begun to feel their effect. The pain in her arm had subsided to a dull throb and the headache that had accompanied her since the accident had begun to fade, as well. But the endless questions in her mind continued.

The EMTs had pressed repeatedly to take her to the hospital for additional observation but she'd finally managed to push them off after submitting to several rounds of "follow the light" as they looked into her eyes, searching for a possible concussion. It had only been Donovan's input—and assurances that he'd keep a watch on her—that had finally quelled the discussion about removing her from the premises.

Not that she exactly wanted to stand around and watch her car smolder in a pile of burned-out metal. Or question who might have wanted to harm her enough to put it in that condition.

It had taken her quite a while to come up with that conclusion, but once she did the sentiment wouldn't shake.

Someone had done this.

Cars didn't just explode when the ignition turned over. And innocent people didn't just get fired from jobs they were good at and loyal to.

So what was going on and what mess had she fallen

into? And had she really left her home that very morning thinking it was just another day?

And how was it that Donovan Colton was the one who arrived to rescue her?

She'd thought of him intermittently over the past five years. Most of the time it was a good memory—a sweet, flirty interlude with an attractive man. But there were other moments—when the memory stung and instead of leaving her with a smile it left her with a strange ache. The painful reminder of what she'd lost that night that went beyond a lost date.

Could things have been different?

In the end it hadn't mattered. If she were honest with herself, it still didn't. Her father was horribly injured that night and her life—all their lives—had irrevocably changed.

"Bellamy?" Gus shuffled up to her, his bright blue eyes hazed with concern. "You've been awfully quiet standing here all by yourself. Are you sure you don't need to go to the emergency room?"

"I'm sure. I'm made of sturdier stuff."

"If you're sure?"

"I'm sure." She glanced at the dissipating crowd. "Did they find any other bombs?"

"It doesn't appear so. The damage from this hooligan seems confined to your car."

Hooligan?

While she had no wish to alarm an old man—and she suspected his use of the word was meant to comfort—the casual term wasn't nearly the correct one for what had happened to her. This wasn't a prank. Or a sick joke. Someone had attempted to kill her. And the sooner she got off of LSP property, the better she'd feel.

"Will I be allowed to go home soon?"

"I overheard Officer Colton talking with the chief. You should be able to get out of here right soon."

"Thanks."

Since her purse had been on her arm when she'd gotten out of the car to close the trunk, she still had many of her personal items. Best of all, she'd been pleased to find her cell phone undamaged where she'd had it zipped in a side pocket. The purse was ripped and headed for the trash but the fact it protected the rest of her personal items was the only saving grace of the evening. Especially seeing as how the car and her small box of memories were destroyed.

"Ms. Reeves?"

Donovan Colton took a commanding spot beside her and Gus, Alex immediately sitting at his side. There was something comforting about the presence of both of them and Bellamy felt a small bit of the stress and strain of the day ebb. "Yes."

"I'd like to ask you a few questions but perhaps you'd prefer to answer them after you've had a chance to clean up. Or maybe eat?"

"You can decide that? I mean, I can leave here."

The edges of his eyes crinkled in a small smile before he nodded. "I think I'm allowed to take you to a more comfortable place and out of the increasing cold. It may be Texas, but it's still December."

She had gotten chilled, the air growing cool once the sun set. "I didn't have lunch and now that you mention it, I am hungry."

"Why don't we leave, then?" Donovan turned to Gus and shook his hand. "You and your team have been incredibly helpful here. Thank you for keeping everyone at the edges and not allowing anyone else to leave until we had a chance to check their cars."

Gus stood taller, his chest puffing just like the dog's. "Of course."

"I'll see that Ms. Reeves is escorted home now. I'll be back tomorrow to finish a review of the site with the chief."

"We'll be waiting for you."

Now that she'd given her agreement to leave, there was little keeping her and Donovan on the property. In a matter of moments, he had her in his SUV and was driving them toward the exit on the back side of the property, in the opposite direction from the press. She wasn't sure if the strategy would work, but refused to turn around to find out.

"I'm sorry for the dog hair. Alex usually sits on the front seat."

A strained giggle crawled up her throat, at odds with the exhaustion that racked her shoulders the moment she sat down. "I think a few stray dog hairs are the least of my worries right now. And since I don't mind them on a good day, it's no bother."

"Are you warm enough?" The heater was on full blast, rapidly warming the car as they drove toward the center of town.

"I'm getting there." As days went, December in central Texas was often mild bordering on warm. She was rarely cold, but since being tossed from the car she'd had a weird, aching numbness that had settled in her bones and refused to let go.

"You're probably dealing with the lingering effects of shock. I should have thought of this sooner. Here."

He pulled to the side of the road and shrugged out of his coat, handing it over. "Put this on."

The jacket enveloped her, a mix of body heat and a scent that was distinctly male. She could still smell the cold air that had wrapped around them in the parking lot, only instead of being tinged with the lingering, acrid taste of smoke and burned-out car, in its place was a musky, pleasing warmth. She also caught the faintest whisper of dog and smiled to herself.

Clearly Alex wasn't at a loss for hugs and affection.

That thought warmed her beyond the car or the coat, filling her with that years-old memory of a large man cradling a sick puppy in his arms. Her father had always told her you could tell a man's character by the way he treated animals and in the case of Donovan Colton, she had to admit the expression was spot on the mark.

"How are you feeling?"

"Better. Warmer." She took in his profile, not wanting to stare but unable to fully look away.

Goodness, was he handsome. She'd thought so that night in her parents' store and saw it even more now. The firm jawline. The close-cropped dark hair. And the thick, corded forearm muscles now visible where he gripped the steering wheel.

"Make a right when you get to the stop sign at the end of this road."

"That's not the way to the diner."

"You don't need to take me to dinner. Home's fine."

"I promised you a meal and I aim to deliver. In fact—" his gaze flashed toward hers before he resumed his focus on the road "—I believe I promised you dinner some time ago."

"That's not... I mean—" She broke off, feeling silly. "I'm covered in parking lot dirt and smell like the undercarriage of a car. Home's fine."

"I'll take you home but I'm not going to leave you right now. You've had an ordeal and I'd like to stick around for a bit."

"I know you have to question me. Can we just do it at my house?"

He frowned before reaching out a hand to lay over hers. "This isn't about questioning you. You're not a criminal, Bellamy. But I will respect your wishes and take you home on one condition."

"What's that?"

"You let me order a pizza from Chuck's."

"How DID A scrappy little guy from Brooklyn end up in Whisperwood, Texas?" Donovan peeked inside the oversize cardboard box of pizza before dropping the lid into place. He'd called in the order as they drove, hoping to minimize their time in town. In retrospect, the decision was a good one when he'd seen a local TV news truck wending its way down Main Street as he pulled away from Chuck's parking lot.

It was too much to hope she wouldn't be found by the press—or worse, whomever had put the bomb in her car—but if he could give her even an evening's peace, then he wanted to do it.

What he hadn't fully reconciled was how much he was looking forward to having dinner with her.

His offered dinner invitation had gone unfulfilled for so many years, it was humbling to realize how anxious he was to see it through. Which was ridiculous because she was now on his caseload and dealing with a horrific trauma.

Bellamy glanced over her shoulder as she grabbed sodas from the fridge before hip bumping the door closed. "Thank Cupid. Chuck met his wife, Maria, on a cruise and decided he couldn't live without her. New York's loss is Whisperwood's gain."

"And Maria's, obviously," Donovan added.

"You seem familiar with the pizza?"

"I'm from here originally. And you don't have to spend much time in Whisperwood before someone makes sure you have a pizza from Chuck's."

While technically true, his mother preferred food cooked in the Colton kitchens by her extensive staff instead of ordering in. Chuck's pizza had been a fortuitous accident one early evening after he'd ducked out of his parents' house and headed home to Austin. Since then, even though he avoided spending a lot of time in Whisperwood, he'd stop off at the small pizzeria after his sporadic visits to his parents' house. He could always make room for a fresh slice and the pizza was almost better the next day, cold, when it came straight out of the fridge.

A small, amused smile tilted Bellamy's lips. "Plates are in the cabinet above the sink."

She stood by her small kitchen table, her dark hair damp from the quick shower he'd encouraged her to take. She was fully dressed, an oversize long-sleeved T-shirt falling over jeans, but something about the look had him doing a double take. There was something fresh about her.

He'd noticed it five years before and was struck anew by that same fact. Even with the horrible events she'd experienced that day, there was a light in her. It had been dampened since their first meeting, but it was still there. Hovering.

Hoping.

Which made the situation she found herself in that much worse. Although he and Alex would go back tomorrow and do a more thorough search of her car, his initial take was that, while deliberate, the bomb had been planted with a degree of amateur crudeness. Crude or not, the work had been effective, the one who planted it only miscalculating the timing device.

And Bellamy's extraordinarily lucky miss by not closing the trunk.

He buried the thought that she was only standing there by the grace of an accident and finished his quick perusal of her, head to toe. It was a skill he'd honed on the job and he used it to his advantage before his gaze alighted on her bare feet. Where he'd have expected her socks to be a soft pink or maybe even a fun red, the distinct shade of burnt orange that covered her toes had him smiling.

"What's that look for?"

He let his gaze linger one more moment on her toes before meeting her eyes. He owed it to her to apprise her of his thoughts on what she was really dealing with, but he wanted time.

Just a bit of time with her.

"It looks like someone's a Longhorn fan."

"As every good graduate of the University of Texas should be." She wiggled the toes on one foot, followed by the other. "I bleed orange, if you must know."

"A pastime around here."

"Pretty much." The mention of her alma mater had

her standing a bit straighter and he was pleased to see a smile persisting on her lips as she crossed the small expanse to the stove. She lifted the lid on the pizza and bent closer to inhale the scent before nodding her head. "Oh yeah. Brooklyn's loss is definitely our gain."

They fixed plates and Bellamy grabbed the two sodas from the counter on their way to a dining alcove just outside the kitchen. The house was modest in size, but cozy, and it was easy to see that she'd made a life for herself here. Her taste wasn't flashy, but he caught subtle hints of whimsy in her home. A superhero cookie jar on the kitchen counter added to the decor and her dining room tablecloth had penguins around the rim.

Alex had laid guard outside the kitchen while they fixed their plates and then repositioned himself after they settled at the table.

"He's so good around food."

"Part of his job."

"It's amazing, though." She shook her head. "I had a dog growing up that made it his business to eat anything he could find, scrounge or flat out steal."

"I had a similar conversation with my mother earlier. I grew up with one of those, too. Alex is special, though. He knows his job and with it, his place."

The flow of casual conversation seemed to do its job. Their easy tumble from topic to topic, from Chuck's love life to the discussion of the Longhorns to ravenous dogs, had left that small, persistent smile on her face.

"Will he eat tonight?"

"I'll feed him when we're done. I keep food in the

car because I never know if we'll be out late. He's working now so he can eat once I'm done."

"Working?"

"Absolutely. You're in his care now. He hasn't taken his eyes off of you."

She laid down her pizza and turned her full attention toward the dog. Although Alex never moved, the tip of his tail started to thump against the floor. "He's watching over me?"

"Yes. Has been ever since we walked over to you in the LSP parking lot. He's going to protect you." *And so am I.*

The thought rang so clearly in his mind he nearly dropped his pizza. Of course it was his job, and by taking the call Bellamy Reeves had absolutely become his responsibility.

But something else called to him.

He had thought about her through the years. The easy moments they'd shared in her parents' store that lone December evening. The sweet way she had with Alex and the quick way she'd leaped to help them.

He'd remembered.

And he'd thought of her every time he'd passed the corner store on his way out of town.

The store had changed hands since then. He was curious about it and was about to ask when she interjected a fresh thought into the conversation.

"I think we get the better end of the deal."

"Of what deal?"

"The human and pet deal. They give us so much and we just sort of take it." As soon as the words were out, she seemed to catch herself. "Not that you treat him poorly—that's not what I meant. But they give from a special place. It's one I don't know humans have."

"I know what you mean. We think we're superior but there's an awful lot we can learn from animals. They live in the moment. They're loyal. And there's an honesty to them that we can't ever hope to aspire to."

"You're smitten."

"With Alex? Definitely."

"He was such a cute puppy and he's grown into such a handsome dog. Is he good at his job?"

"The best."

"Let me amend my earlier comment. You're smitten *and* biased."

The lightest whisper of heat crawled up his neck. "I suppose I am. He really is good, though. He consistently wins the drills we run across the K-9 teams. And he's got a special sort of alertness. Like now. He looks like he's casually sitting there but he's totally focused on the two of us and on his surroundings."

"What was your takeaway of today?"

The shift in question caught him off guard and Donovan couldn't help thinking that Bellamy Reeves was totally aware of her surroundings, too.

And the danger that threatened her in ways he couldn't begin to imagine.

BELLAMY WANTED TO hover in the warm cocoon of her house and her most comfy clothes and the incredibly able strength of Officer Donovan Colton and his sidekick, Alex. More, she wanted to lose herself in all of it and shut out whatever lurked outside her door.

Which was the very reason she had to ask the question. And accept that the darkness that came into Dono-

van's already dark brown gaze had nothing to do with
her question and everything to do with the answer.

Something terrible had happened today and pre-
tending it hadn't wasn't going to set her up very well.

Just like her parents.

Where her sister had been insistent in believing
things weren't "that bad" after the accident, Bellamy
had pressed on, well aware of what difficult times faced
them. Her father's resulting paralysis—and the diffi-
culty of trying to have a seventy-five-year-old body
bounce back against that sort of crushing destruction—
was nearly impossible.

And she'd met it head-on.

She hadn't hid, nor had she run.

Then why was the urge to do so now so overwhelming and urgent?

And what was she going to do about what she'd
found?

"My takeaway?"

She nodded. "I know you haven't written a formal
report, but you've obviously done this for some time.
What was your initial impression?"

"I still need to question you. I also need to share my
thoughts with my commanding officer."

"I see."

And just like that, he went into cop mode, shutting
her out of what was clearly her own problem to deal
with. Just like the doctors. Just like her sister. Hell,
even just like her mother.

Life had careened out of control once again and the
only person left to manage it was her.

Standing, she took her empty plate into the kitchen
and placed everything in the sink. The rich scents of

tomato sauce and cheese still wafted from the closed cardboard but she'd suddenly lost her appetite.

It was unfair to paint Donovan with the same brush as others in her life—she hadn't even told him of the email yet or the events of the day—but his reticence to share with her still stung.

"Bellamy, I'm sorry." She wasn't surprised he'd followed her, but she was stunned to feel the wall of heat that emanated against her back. "I'm not trying to keep you in the dark."

"Spare me."

"It's my job and I need to report my thoughts to my boss. I owe it to him. But that doesn't mean I won't tell you what I know. Nor does it mean I'm going to keep you in the dark. But I need to follow the correct chain of command and management of evidence."

"Evidence?"

"Your car is evidence. That's what I asked the chief to move into police custody. Alex and I will look at it tomorrow and we'll have a better sense of what we're dealing with."

That wall of heat seemed to grow warmer, if possible, even though he didn't touch her. Despite the lack of contact, she could feel him. Could practically sense the beat of his heart.

And even as she hated being kept in the dark, she couldn't deny how good it felt to have him stand there. To have him in her home, filling up the space.

To have someone nearby.

"I won't keep you in the dark. But please let me do my job."

"I got fired today." The words slipped out, as embarrassing to say them out loud as they'd been to digest in Sally Borne's office.

"What for?"

"Reporting an email I wasn't supposed to have received in the first place." She reached for a nearby dish towel, twisting the material beneath her fingers. "Or maybe I was. Who knows?"

Large hands settled on her shoulders, lingering there briefly before turning her around. "What's this about? I need you to tell me. Tell me all of it."

She knew this moment was inevitable. Had even expected it as she'd worked to process all that had happened since opening that stupid email earlier.

What she hadn't expected were the tears. Hot and sharp, they filled her eyes and tightened her throat like fingers wrapped around her neck. Worse, once she let them out, there was no way to pull them back.

"I—" She swallowed the hiccup, even as another hard sob swamped her.

And then it didn't matter. There was no need for words or explanations or even apologies as Donovan pulled her against that broad, capable, gloriously strong chest. He held her there, his arms around her and his hand nestled against her head where he stroked her hair, seeing her through the uncontrollable rush of emotion and raw adrenaline that finally had a place to land.

Sobs racked her frame as the hot tears continued to pour, unchecked, from her eyes. Abstractly, she thought to be embarrassed, but the sheer relief of expelling all that pent-up emotion kept her from dwelling on anything for too long.

As the tears finally subsided, those lingering moments of embarrassment bubbled to the surface. On a hiccup, she looked up at him, attempting to slip from his hold. "I am sorry."

He didn't budge, a wall of heat and man and solid strength. "Don't go anywhere."

"I...I mean... I—" A horrified squeak fell from her lips as she realized she stood in her kitchen, crying her eyes out in front of a virtual stranger. "I'm so sorry."

"Don't be sorry. And while you're at it, forget embarrassed, anxious or silly. You had a bad day. A really bad day. This will help you start to feel better."

As pep talks went, his admonishments did the trick. The embarrassment was already fading and in its place came that subtle tug of attraction her body still remembered from all those years ago.

Donovan Colton was an impressive man, and not just for the solid physique and commanding presence. The man had layers. She'd sensed it five years ago and she sensed it now, even as she had no reason for the observation.

Yet something was there.

Her mother had always teased her about being borderline psychic but she'd never paid it much mind. Bellamy had always believed instead it meant taking the time to observe her surroundings. She wasn't shy, per se, but she wasn't the first person to leap in and begin talking. Rather, she appreciated the opportunity to sit and observe before being called on to say anything.

Appreciated the opportunity to get her bearings around people.

The side benefit was that she'd learned to read people. She'd developed a sense of what made them tick and, often, what motivated them.

And that's where Donovan Colton tripped her up. It

was obvious he was crazy about his dog. Along with that she took him at face value as a good, honorable cop. Even his reticence to share his thoughts on her case were steeped in following protocol, which she could—and did—respect.

So why the subtle sense that he was almost desperate to prove his place in the world?

She'd thought it earlier when he'd spoken of the pizza. He might be from Whisperwood but there was a distinct note of dissonance, that he clearly felt he didn't belong here. Nor did he have much love for his hometown. Again, she couldn't define how she knew that, she simply did.

"Are you all right now?" Donovan asked.

"Yeah. I feel better."

"Do you want anything else to eat?"

"No." She rubbed her stomach, the crying jag having left her raw and hollowed out. "I'm good."

"You mind if I feed Alex, then? And we can talk after."

"Go ahead."

Donovan ducked out of the kitchen and after some murmured words to Alex, she heard her front door click shut. Alex trotted into the kitchen in the wake of his master's departure, his tail wagging and his gentle brown eyes alert as he took her in.

"You're such a pretty boy." Bellamy picked up a plastic bowl she'd filled for him earlier and freshened the water. His nails tapped on her hardwood floor as he walked over to the bowl, his gaze on her until he dropped his head to the water and drank his fill.

Even in something so simple and natural, she knew the dog was alert and keen to his surroundings. What fascinated her was how attuned he was to her. It didn't take much to know Donovan's directive to the animal had been to watch over her. What she didn't know was what she was going to do when they had to leave.

Or how she'd fight back against the inevitable threat when it came at her once more.

Chapter Four

While Alex dived into his dinner, Donovan left his partner to his food and walked back into the dining room. Bellamy stood arrow straight, her head slightly bowed as her hands trailed over a small sideboard. She stared down at a series of photos and even from where he stood he could see she focused on one in particular.

"Are those your parents?"

"Yes." She tapped one of the photos. "This was their fiftieth anniversary."

He did the quick math in his head, surprised to realize they had been so old. "Do you have a lot of brothers and sisters?"

"No, just me and my younger sister, Magnolia. Maggie," she quickly added.

"Then your parents were older when they had children? Because there's no way you're close to fifty."

She turned away from the photo, the aimless energy that seemed to grip her at the sideboard fading as he asked her about her life. "Yes. And that photo was taken about six years ago. Before my father—" She hesitated, then continued, "Before his health declined. My mother's followed on the heels of that."

"I'm sorry for that."

And he was. While Donovan took full credit for the personal challenges he had with his own family, he loved them. It had been hard to see his father struggle the past couple of years as he was naturally forced to slow down from his normal routine—racing around the ranch, flying places for his business interests or evenings out entertaining. And his mother, for all her bright and happy chatter, carried the burdens of age, as well. She'd let go of a few commitments over the past few years, preferring events that didn't have her driving at night.

He supposed it was the natural order of things, but it didn't mean it hadn't been a transition.

"What about you?" Bellamy asked. "Any brothers or sisters?"

"Oh, the Colton family is a prolific one. I'm one of four, all older than me, and I come from a family that's even larger."

"That must be nice."

"Most of the time." Donovan avoided mentioning when it wasn't, especially since he had relatives who'd both spent time in jail for heinous crimes. While he knew his extended family didn't reflect on him, he was well aware there were places in Texas and beyond where the Colton name didn't win any fans.

How funny, then, that his parents were the antithesis. They'd been more than willing to take him in, nearly falling over themselves to make him part of the family. To save him, that poor little abandoned soul, dropped into their midst.

"You don't like coming from a big family?"

I don't like feeling like an outsider with all those eyes watching.

He never had. But like the black sheep branch of his family, he refused to mention anything. Instead, he focused on the positive and the values his mother had impressed upon him.

"It has its moments. I can do without everyone being in each other's business. But it is nice knowing I have so many people to count on."

Her gaze flitted back to the photos at the edge of the sideboard before shifting determinedly back to him. "People to count on. That must be nice."

Alex trotted into the room, his dinner at an end and his guard duties back in place as he took a seat facing the two of them. The overwhelming events of the day—and the danger that lurked beneath—still seemed like a dream. Because she wanted to keep it that way for a few hours more, Bellamy focused on the dog. "I should probably let you both go. I'll be fine for tonight and then I can come in and make a statement tomorrow, if that's okay? I'm suddenly not up for getting into a recounting of my afternoon once again."

Exhaustion rode Bellamy's features, with dark smudges settling beneath her eyes postcrying jag. He didn't want to leave her but he hardly had a reason to stay, either. "I'm scheduled to meet with the chief tomorrow morning at ten. I would like to get your statement before then."

"How about if I come into the station at eight?" A hard laugh escaped her chest. "It's not like I have to go into work, after all."

She'd mentioned the job earlier, right before she was overcome with the emotions of the day. "You sure you don't want to talk about it now?"

"Can it wait? I promise I'll tell you everything. Including anything that may become clearer overnight."

"You have a deal, then."

"Oh. Wait." The bum's rush wasn't lost on him, so he was surprised when she stopped him. "I don't have a car."

"Alex and I can swing by and pick you up. I'll even include a stop at the coffee place in town."

"You don't have to—"

He reached for her hand, the move meant to reassure, but the sudden stop of her words hung heavy between them.

"It's okay. I can give you a hand. And it's not like Whisperwood is this sprawling metropolis. You're like a two-minute detour after I turn into town."

"Okay, then."

In moments she had him bustled out her front door, the rest of the pizza in his hands. As he opened the door of his SUV for Alex to hop in, Donovan couldn't avoid the impressions that had bombarded him over the past few hours. Where he'd initially seen a woman dealing with a difficult circumstance, those moments when she stared at her photos suggested something else.

Something more.

Bellamy Reeves was a lonely woman. And if his instincts were correct, she was dealing with something far beyond her understanding.

JENSEN TAYLOR SCROLLED impatiently through the news articles on his tablet, hunting for anything that might mention the incident in the parking lot at LSP. His father, Sutton, had been touch and go in the hospital for the past few weeks, a private matter Jensen had deliberately kept from the employees at LSP, but the old man had rallied over the past few days.

He'd inevitably be fielding phone calls if Sutton caught wind of a bomb detonating in the LSP parking lot.

He and his father did well keeping their distance— emotional and, when Jensen could manage it, physical— and the hospital stay had helped that even more. Jensen saw no reason to change that. He played the devoted son when it was warranted and then went about living his life the rest of the time. Now that Jensen's mother was dead, the situation worked well for them both.

Of course, cars blowing up in the LSP parking lot were likely to draw the old man's attention, no matter how poorly he felt. His father had been lingering at a private facility south of Austin, but he hadn't died. Public problems at LSP might give Sutton the ammunition to recover fully and that was the last thing Jensen needed.

All he had to do was convince the old man he had it under control.

It was his only choice.

He had little interest—actually, make that *no* interest—in pharmaceuticals, but he'd be damned if any of his father's bastards would get a piece of his legacy. The old man had already suggested he wanted to open up a new position on the leadership team for the moment one of his brats finished business school.

Oh, that was a big, Texas-sized *hell no*.

This was the only way to manage things and ensure his father's far-too-generous heart didn't ruin Jensen's future.

The entire situation had a funny sort of justice to

it. His father had always played the field, his simpering mother just living with it while she flitted around as society matron of their hick town. Then his mother died and instead of publicly playing the field after an appropriate mourning period, poor Sutton was all sick and weak.

Justice at its finest.

LSP might have turned Whisperwood into one of the largest suburbs outside of Austin but it was still central Texas. Small freaking potatoes. But that hadn't stopped his father. The man had worked his playboy magic from one end of the Hill Country to the other. His mother had ignored it all, seeming to believe all that mattered was the large house Sutton had built for her, visible to anyone who drove a few blocks off of Whisperwood's main drag.

They really were a pair.

Jensen hadn't spent much time worrying if the two of them loved each other, but he had taken a few notes for himself on the type of woman who'd make a good partner. He could do with one who had his mother's penchant for living in ignorant bliss. Sadly, the last few women he'd dated hadn't fit the bill.

Resigned to worry about it later, Jensen shot a quick email to his father, assuring him all was well and to continue to rest and focus on getting better.

"Wanted you to hear it from me. Absolutely nothing to worry about. A holiday prank gone bad," Jensen muttered as he typed up a quick note and shot it off. He'd know by morning if the old man had bought it.

In the meantime, he wanted to do a bit of digging.

And figure out just what Bellamy Reeves knew.

BELLAMY GATHERED HER hair up in a twist, clipping the dark brown mass. Then she added a few quick swipes of mascara to her eyes for good measure. She'd spent a restless night and was well aware there was no amount of makeup that could cover the bags beneath her eyes.

"More like potato sacks," she acknowledged to herself as she added one last swipe of the mascara wand.

Standing back to assess her image in the mirror, she was pleased to see the mascara had at least made her look a bit more human. Zombie TV shows might be popular but no one wanted a monster walking down the Main Street of Whisperwood at eight in the morning.

The lack of a car was a problem, but she'd deal with that after she made her statement to Donovan. She'd already logged in the night before and started the claim process with her insurance company. The automated email she got back confirmed someone would call her today to keep the process moving.

Making one final effort to look human with a pass of her lip gloss, she grabbed a light jacket from her closet and went to wait in the front room for Donovan. The oppressive weight of the day before faded a bit as she thought about the strong, capable man and his dog.

They were an impressive pair. The dog was both obedient and clearly in love with his master, the big eyes and devoted stare something to see. She couldn't stop the small smile at the image they made, the affection in Donovan's eyes for the large black Lab proof he was equally smitten. It was sweet to see. And made a good-looking man even more attractive.

Along with her dad's advice, she'd also read once on a dating blog that three signs to watch for in a prospective mate were how they behaved with waiters, how they spoke in conflict and how they treated animals. From what she could see, Donovan Colton passed all three tests with flying colors.

It had been one of the things she still remembered about that night so long ago when he'd come into the store with a sweet little puppy. That mix of concern and care for an animal was an obvious clue to his personality.

Unbidden, the rest of that long-ago evening filled her thoughts. The easy conversation and subtle flirtation. Even the clear stamp of interest in his gaze. She'd been more interested than she could describe and had wanted to see him again.

Of course, all that had been forgotten once the news of her parents' accident was delivered. And all that had come after had changed her life in ways she never could have imagined.

So how odd that he was back. That he was the one who'd been in Whisperwood and taken the call for her car. And that he was the one she'd now share her story with.

Engine sounds purred from her driveway and a glance out the front window indicated her chariot had arrived. She picked up her things and let herself out of the house, surprised when either Donovan or Alex were nowhere in sight.

"Donovan?" When he didn't answer she hollered. "Donovan!"

His voice was muffled but came back from the opposite side of the yard. "Be right there! Stay at the door."

She stood still, curious to where he and his K-9 partner vanished to, but willing to follow the direction. She was nearly ready to go looking for them when Donovan reached her just as she was turning the key in the lock.

"Good morning, Bellamy."

"Oh!" She'd expected to meet him at the car, so the large frame and imposing presence was a surprise. "You didn't have to... I mean, I could have come to you."

"This is door-to-door service, ma'am. Even when I make you wait while Alex and I check the perimeter." He smiled and mimed tipping an imaginary hat. "It's part of the Texas gentleman's code."

She swallowed hard around the idea her perimeter even required checking and opted for a shot of dark humor. "The Texas gentleman's code? Is that a euphemism for politely escorting a suspect to the police station?"

The moment the words were out of her mouth, she knew they'd missed the mark. The anxiety that had kept her company throughout a restless night—including the fear that something horrible at LSP was somehow being blamed on her—had taken root and wouldn't let go.

But it was the frown that marred his face—matched to an equally disappointed light in his eyes—that had her rethinking the remark.

"This is nothing but routine."

"It may be for you, but it's not every day my car blows up and I follow it up with a visit to the police to make a statement."

"Did you do it?"

"What?" The sheer shock his question gave her had her mouth dropping, her momentary concern at possibly offending him fading away. "You think I did that?

To my car? To my stuff? Why would I do that? And possibly kill myself in the process?"

Donovan had already walked her to his SUV, his expression turning serious as he put his hand on the car door handle. "I don't think anything of the sort. Or I'm trying hard not to, even though my instincts as a cop are to question everything."

"So you do think I did it?" The words came out prim and stiff and she wanted to sink through the driveway at the small shot of hurt that burrowed beneath her breast.

"I'm asking questions. Just like the chief will do. Just like reporters will do. Keep that hot core of righteous anger and you'll be just fine."

Bellamy was about to reply when Donovan pulled the door open. Alex was already in the back seat and she could see the depression marks of a sweeper head over the entire seat, from the back panel to the portion where she'd rest in her neatly pressed clothes. "You vacuumed?"

"Of course. I love Alex but I'm well aware no one wants to wear him."

"But… I mean…" She stopped, the weird conversation and the added awkwardness of her reaction to his questions slowing her down. She climbed into the SUV seat, but laid a hand on his arm before he could close the door. "Why don't I try this again? Good morning, Donovan. It's nice to see you. Thank you for picking me up."

He smiled once more, a small dimple winking in his cheek when the corners of his lips tilted upward into a relaxed grin. "Good morning, Bellamy. It's my pleasure."

He closed the door and she watched him walk around the front of the SUV, more than willing to look her fill unnoticed. He was still as attractive as that night he'd come into her parents' store, but he'd aged, as well. The rounder cheeks that marked a younger man were gone, replaced with a slight hollowing beneath the bones that set off his features. His jaw seemed harder than she remembered and there was a solidness to his frame that was rougher. Worn.

No, she amended to herself, *experienced*.

Age worked itself on every person in a myriad of ways, but experience left a different sort of mark. It stamped itself on the body by way of bearing and attitude, words and gestures.

He fascinates me.

The words popped into her mind, unbidden, but she gave them room to grow and the space to breathe.

Donovan Colton did fascinate her. He was attractive, obviously, but there was more. And what seemed to tug at her the most was what she sensed lay beneath the surface.

Unaware of her close scrutiny, Donovan hopped into the car and turned toward her. "Coffee first?"

"Sure."

"Then here." He reached behind his seat and pulled a cardboard container from the floor. "I didn't know what you liked but figured I couldn't go wrong with a latte."

"Thanks. And you guessed right."

The scent of coffee drifted from the cup in her hand and she wondered that she hadn't smelled it the moment she got into the car.

"You've been busy this morning. First the vacuum.

Then the coffee. Did you catch a few bad guys while you were at it?"

"Alex and I are early risers. And I wanted to beat the traffic out of Austin so it worked."

"You didn't just stay at your parents'?"

"No."

Although she'd fumbled her first few comments, she'd gotten them back on track once she took her seat. For that reason, it was surprising to see his gaze shutter so tightly at the mention of his family. Her mother had always teased her that she was intuitive, but she didn't need a lick of extra awareness to know that there was a no-trespassing sign on Donovan's relationship with his parents.

What she wanted to know was why.

The Coltons were well-known in Whisperwood and throughout the greater Austin area. She had been so busy with her own family the past few years she hadn't paid a ton of attention to community gossip, but she wasn't completely immune, either.

She knew of the Coltons. To Donovan's comments the prior evening, he came from a large clan, with several branches spread across the state. The Colton family had been in the news recently, in fact, when serial criminal Livia Colton had escaped from prison. Public knowledge or not, it seemed bad form to mention that, so she relied on the manners her mother had drilled in from childhood and changed the subject.

"I know Austin's not that far. And it's always nice to sleep in your own bed."

"Exactly."

Donovan started the car, the weird moment seemingly forgotten as he navigated down her street and to-

ward the main road into town. At a loss over what to
say, Bellamy twisted in her seat, petting and praising
Alex as she told him good morning.

Energy quivered beneath the dog's fur but he held
his position in the back seat. She ran her fingers over
the extra soft areas behind his ear, finding a sensitive
spot that had his eyelids dimming in pleasure.

It was so simple, she marveled to herself. So easy.
Alex wanted praise, attention and a reason to give his
trust.

As Donovan's evasion over his family ran once more
through her mind, she acknowledged to herself that
people were far more difficult to figure out.

DONOVAN MADE THE turn into the parking lot at the
Whisperwood police station. Bellamy had kept up a
steady conversation on the short drive from her house,
but quieted as they turned into town. The air seemed
to shift and Donovan saw Alex shift with it, his already straight posture going even stiffer where he stood
guard in the back seat.

Unable to delay the discussion, Donovan instead
chose to treat it with the same casual care he'd managed at her house. This wasn't designed to be an in-
terrogation, but they did need to understand what had
happened to her and why Bellamy was targeted. He'd
already sent the materials he'd collected on scene at
LSP to the bomb squad and would oversee their review personally.

But none of that would assuage her anxiety or make
this morning's discussion any easier.

Chief Archer Thompson greeted them personally,
authority stamped in his bearing. In moments he had

them seated in his office, his own coffee in hand. Donovan liked Archer. He was a good guy, took the law seriously and had always been a collaborative partner. The man reinforced that belief in the way he set up the conversation and explained to Bellamy what they needed to understand.

"Ms. Reeves, thank you for coming in today."

"Of course." She nodded and while her shoulders were still set in a stiff line, her hand no longer clenched her coffee cup in a death grip, which Donovan took for an improvement.

"I'm going to ask you several questions and some of them I'm going to ask more than once to see if you remember things from a different perspective."

"I understand."

With her head nod, Archer started. He took her basic information, even how long she'd been in Whisperwood, peppering in pleasant comments along the way and easing her into the discussion. Although Donovan knew his way around an interview, the ease with which Arch managed the conversation was impressive.

"How long have you been at Lone Star Pharmaceutical?" Archer asked.

"For a little over thirteen years. I started with them out of college."

Donovan digested that point. Thirteen years in her profession put her around thirty-five if she did college in the standard timing. He was thirty-one and had estimated her to be around the same age, so it was intriguing to know she had a few years on him.

You'd do better with an older woman, Donovan. You're far too serious for a younger woman to stay interested.

His sister had said that to him recently and he'd been amused and vaguely offended. Too serious? Since she was kind to a fault, he quickly saw his way past it, but the underlying intention in his sister's thoughts had stuck.

He had dated younger and none of those relationships—for the ones that could even be called a full-on relationship—had had much life in them. He had Alex and his work and while the initial weeks of a relationship went well, the moment things turned serious and his schedule wasn't fully aligned to theirs, the women he dated chose to walk.

Bellamy Reeves didn't strike him as a woman who walked. From what she described of her parents' needs, she had stuck around, taking care of them and seeing to their well-being. She'd been loyal to a job when far more people were jumping from company to company for greener pastures. Even the night they'd met, she'd been at the store helping out.

It was an impressive trait, one he couldn't deny appealed to him.

Hell, Colton, might as well just suck it up and admit it. Everything about the woman appeals to you.

"Did anything unusual stand out about your day yesterday?"

Donovan keyed back into Archer's questions, the basic pleasantries of job history and life in Whisperwood long past.

"The whole day was unusual."

"Did something happen?" Archer leaned forward, his already sharp focus growing visibly more pointed. "Something besides the car?"

"It was… Well, I mean, I found something. On

email." Her fingers fumbled as she reached for her purse where she'd set it beside her. "I have an email. I printed a few copies."

Archer kept his cop's eyes focused on her purse, his attention unwavering until she pulled the promised piece of paper from her bag. Although Donovan had no qualms her purse held nothing more than what she'd said, he couldn't blame the man for staying on his guard.

If she sensed the heightened attention, Bellamy never indicated it, instead handing over a piece of paper folded in half. She handed a second copy to Donovan and he quickly read through the terse, telling statements, bulleted out in list form after a cold, lifeless salutation.

Donovan scanned the page again, his gaze going to the header that had printed out along with the content of the note. Her name was printed in the "To" line, along with her full email address, but no named sender was visible in the "From" line, just the word INTERNAL. The date was yesterday, the timing late morning as she'd already shared.

He wasn't an expert in technology and programming, but he had enough working knowledge to know something was manipulated in the note. A masked sender was a problem.

A problem that could be easily created if one simply altered a printout.

The thought struck fast and hard, nearly knocking his breath. His gaze shot to Archer's and he saw the chief had already traveled down that path and fast.

"Ms. Reeves. Tell me a bit more about this email. Do you know if anyone else received one?"

"I think it was only me but I don't know. We're on a lighter work schedule with the holidays so there were fewer people around. Not that it would have mattered." She shrugged, her vivid gray eyes dulled with the troubling memories of the day before. "I didn't go around asking anyone. I thought it was wrong to do that until I'd spoken to Human Resources."

"And what did they say?"

"They fired me."

"Yesterday?" the chief clarified, before pointing to the lone sheet of paper in his hands. "After you reported this email to them?"

"Yes, that's correct."

"Based on what you've described, you're a loyal employee."

"I thought so, too. But I wasn't even given a chance to explain. HR refused to support me or even listen to my side of the story."

"Have you been working on any special projects? Anything that would have given you access to the details in this email?"

"Of course not. That email's about price-fixing, market manipulation and harming our customers. If LSP did that, I'd have quit on my own a long time ago."

"So this is a malicious rumor, then? Something to harm the company."

Bellamy stilled at the suggestion, her eyes going wide. "This is a terrible rumor to go spreading. It could ruin the company."

"I agree," Archer said.

Donovan had remained quiet, allowing the chief to do his work, but he couldn't stay silent any longer. "Do you know who sent this? Someone who had a vendetta against the company? A disgruntled employee or maybe someone else let go recently?"

"I don't know anyone who'd do this. LSP is a reputable company. I've worked in the finance department for thirteen years. We file our reports properly and on time. We manage all government requirements and standards the industry is held to. Nothing about this email, or the practices it suggests, makes any sense. Too many people would know if something like this was happening. LSP provides vaccines to the entire Southwest. You don't just cover up something like this."

"Then it does sound like a vicious rumor designed to seed doubt and destroy the company's reputation."

"Maybe. I don't know."

"Don't you, Ms. Reeves?" Archer left the thought hanging, the impression of an affable, easygoing town leader fading in the space of a heartbeat. "Because it would be easy enough to manipulate a printout like this. Even easier for someone with such a lauded history at the company to whisper to a few people and seed a whole lot of doubt."

"You think I did this? Me?" Her voice squeaked on the last word.

"I have to ask those questions. It's my job."

Whatever nervousness carried her into Archer Thompson's office vanished as Bellamy rose from her chair. She stood tall, her gaze direct as she stared the chief down across his desk.

The same alertness that had filled Archer's eyes returned, matched by Alex's sudden readiness beside Donovan. They all seemed to hang there, the moment stretching out in a weird tableau of mismatched power, authority and frustration.

"I lost my job yesterday, Chief Thompson. In the span of an afternoon, I lost my professional home, my reputation and nearly my life. I don't know what sort of cruel, vicious game someone's playing with me but I did not write this email, nor did I manipulate its contents."

"No one's suggesting you did."

"Oh no? I came in here to freely discuss what happened and in moments, you managed to make me feel as if I was responsible for this." She shook her own copy of the email, the one she'd retained for herself. "I'm lucky I even printed this out, but it was a last-minute thought before I blithely marched down to Human Resources, thinking they could help me. Or at minimum listen to my concerns and give me a fair shot. But they failed me and now so have you." She sat back down, her gaze remaining steady before it flicked over to him. "Both of you."

Donovan wanted to argue but said nothing. She wasn't wrong.

And he had failed her. He'd promised her a safe space and instead had brought her into the lion's den.

Bellamy's gaze returned to the chief, her attention so focused Donovan might have left for all she'd have noticed. That same loneliness he'd sensed the night before was back, her posture shuttered and protective as she turned fully in her chair to face Archer.

"Ask me whatever you want, Chief Thompson. Ask me however many ways you want to. The truth remains the same."

Chapter Five

Bellamy couldn't get out of there fast enough. She'd walked into Chief Thompson's office a trusting soul and walked out disappointed and once again unsure of herself. Why had she even listened to Donovan Colton in the first place? Had she really been taken in by the big, bad protector routine? The hot cop with the cute dog.

Was she really that lame? Or that hard up?

Obviously she was both.

With the interview at an end, she'd already left the chief's office a free woman.

For now, that small, scared voice inside whispered. She'd done her level best to keep it quiet, but she couldn't deny the raw, mind-numbing fear or the surreal nightmare she seemed to have fallen into, like Dorothy into Munchkinland. Why didn't anyone believe her? Or, at minimum, listen to her without judgment?

Was LSP so powerful that no one believed anything could happen there? That an employee could possibly discover something that was at best below standard and at worst, nefarious and deliberate?

Even as she asked herself the questions, she knew

the truth. Had it been anyone else, she'd have questioned them, too.

What really stung was Donovan. She'd placed her already fragile trust in him and what had she gotten for it?

Just like Maggie.

Her hands fumbled as she stood in the lobby of the Whisperwood police station, punching a request for a car into an app on her phone.

Like Maggie?

Whatever this situation might be, it was nothing like her relationship with her sister. Nothing at all.

Maggie had left her and their parents when they needed her most. Instead of providing the familial support and understanding their family needed, Maggie had chosen a life with her rich new husband, James, and came around as little as possible.

Bellamy had given Maggie the benefit of the doubt at first. Newlyweds should have a chance to start their marriage off right, spending time with each other and cementing their relationship. She'd said those words to her mother often, especially on the occasions when Maggie turned down invitations to Sunday dinner or couldn't come by the hospital when her father got too sick, disabled beyond her ability to care for him. She'd been adamant that her sister needed that time until the day she realized she was adrift at sea, caring for her parents all by herself.

It had been those times that had created the rift that had never mended.

Get out of there, Bell. They're suffocating you.

They're our parents. How can you even suggest that? Worse, how can you walk away?

I'm not walking away. I'm talking about legitimate care that can handle Dad's needs and whatever it is that's got Mom fading away more and more every day.

They're my parents.

They're my *parents, too. Yet you've done nothing I've asked. You refuse to even listen to reason.*

The conversation had changed as their father's condition worsened, but only about where her parents should be for the optimal care. As if it mattered. The type of facility her father belonged in wasn't anything they could have afforded, even if they'd wanted to. So Bellamy had scraped together what she could for daytime care and had swallowed her pride and taken her sister's husband's money to fill in the gaps.

And they'd gotten by. Her father might not have had perfect care, but he had his family around him and he'd lived in his own home. The house was small, so it hadn't been too difficult to make the needed changes to help him get around. And they'd all gotten used to the hospital bed in the front room after a while.

The images were still so vivid, yet at times they seemed like another lifetime, they were so distant. The house had become hers after her parents' life insurance settlement and it no longer resembled the home of an invalid. Wheelchairs, hospital beds and the endless rows of pills were long gone. The scent of illness no longer lingered.

At times she was relieved and at others she wished she could bring it all back, would do whatever it took to have even one more day.

When she went to her last physical in September, her doctor had told her these swings in emotion were the natural cycle of grief. Even knowing that didn't make the days easier or the memories any less weighty.

The ping of her phone announcing the arrival of her driver pulled her from the maudlin thoughts. She'd fought so hard not to be a martyr over her parents, so it was disheartening to realize how quickly those feelings could creep in, especially when she thought about Maggie.

It was negative energy and she didn't want it or need it in her life. Just like she didn't need to be the object of a criminal investigation into why she might have decided to blow herself up.

As if.

Shaking it all off, she got into the car that pulled up to the curb. For as small as they were, even Whisperwood had adopted personalized transportation apps and she'd never been more pleased about that. She'd get home on her own and could assess the damage from her kitchen table.

With the police station firmly behind her, Bellamy focused on the driver's route through town and toward her small home.

Her haven.

She'd hole up and assess the damage.

And then she was going to figure out just what the hell was going on and why she'd somehow been targeted as the one to take the fall.

"THAT WENT WELL." Chief Thompson stared at the closed office door in the direction Bellamy just departed.

"Please tell me that's your special brand of sarcasm." Donovan eyed Alex where he lay on the floor across the room and could have sworn the animal let out a small sniff of displeasure.

"Justice may be blind but I'm not. If that woman's guilty, I'll eat my hat."

Donovan thought the same but was curious about Archer's sudden assessment. "You didn't act like she was innocent."

"Appearances. I can't have my constituents thinking I'm soft or unable to ask the tough questions. But there was some pure, righteous anger there the moment the tone changed. She was well and rightly pissed at both of us and I'm glad. She's going to need that bit of fire to get through whatever is going on here."

"You believe the email?"

"No reason not to."

Donovan glanced down at the paper he still held in a tight grip. "Emails can be doctored."

"Lots of things can be doctored. What I don't see in this situation is why. She's got a good job. She's well liked and well respected. I did some preliminary digging. She's not in debt or trouble and there's nothing to suggest she's got some sort of vendetta and is looking to ruin Lone Star Pharmaceutical. Nothing clicks there."

"No, it doesn't."

It didn't make any more sense an hour later as Donovan worked over Bellamy's car. The chief had had her vehicle towed to a small impound area the man kept for police business and Donovan had gone straight there with Alex after leaving the station. Her gray gaze still haunted him, the whispers of "traitor" and "coconspirator" stamped so clearly in those depths they might as well have been written out.

And hadn't he contributed to that?

He'd brought Bellamy to the station himself, hand delivered to the front door. He'd genuinely believed she was the victim in this situation, but the moment she'd pulled out that email the tenor of the meeting had changed. Archer might be working the bad cop routine but that didn't exactly leave Donovan as good cop.

And he still had questions.

Was Bellamy responsible in any way for what had happened? And if she wasn't, then why was she targeted with such incriminating information?

Worse, what sort of scam was LSP running against the market?

The chief had promised to start looking into those elements, especially since the case was on his turf, but Donovan knew well that wasn't an easy investigation for anyone, let alone a small police department that had grown on the goodwill and funding of the town's largest employer.

Donovan had almost used that level of conflict to transfer the investigation to his own precinct in Austin when Archer took matters into his own hands. The chief sent all notes and information to the Austin PD chief himself, CC-ing Donovan in the process.

Nothing about this situation made any sense. Instead, it felt like mysteries wrapped in mysteries, with no discernable threads or entry points.

By all indications, Bellamy Reeves was a solid, well-respected employee. Responsible, but not a part of the company's upper echelon. And yet she'd somehow been granted access to information that created a quagmire of doubt.

What could she possibly know?

If she were higher up in LSP, he might explore a whistle-blower angle, but she didn't have the power to affect that sort of change.

Shaking his head to dislodge the roiling thoughts, Donovan caught sight of Alex from the corner of his eye. The dog was still seated in the position he'd instructed, his gaze never wavering as Donovan searched the car with a flashlight.

Was that accusation he saw in his partner's eyes?

Alex had been his usual obedient self, but he'd deliberately sniffed the front passenger seat of the car before they climbed in and headed for the impound lot. He'd also taken the back seat, refusing to sit in his normal spot in the front.

Loyalty to Bellamy?

If it was, he'd take Alex's judgment more seriously than many others.

But even with the positive canine reinforcement, it didn't change the situation. Bellamy Reeves was in a heap of trouble.

"It's about damn time you figured out why, Colton."

Whether it was the muttered instructions or the simple twist of a moment, he had no idea, but his flashlight tilted over a quick glint of something lightly colored. Repositioning the light, he searched once more for the source and saw a small, thin button, the sort used on men's fancy dress shirts. He flashed the light fully on the object, a momentary pang that a man might have lost a button in Bellamy's car burning through him like wildfire.

The woman *was* entitled to date. To have relationships. Hell, she could make out in her damn car if she wanted to, buttons flying in all directions in the heat of the moment. What business was it of his?

At the bark from behind him, Donovan turned to see Alex, that firm stare still in place. "Okay, fine. No jumping to conclusions."

Even as the odd shot of jealousy lingered, Donovan refocused on the evidence he'd collected. He carefully picked up the button with his gloved hand, anxious to preserve whatever prints might be on the flat disc as part of the investigation. After dropping it into an evidence bag from his field kit, he stood back to assess the car once more.

With a light pat on his thigh, he motioned Alex closer and was comforted when that large body scrambled to join him, resettling himself at Donovan's side. Together they stared at the remains of the car.

It was a simple, serviceable sedan, about four years old. Nothing flashy, but it had been kept clean. Even beneath the grit and residue of the explosion, he could see there weren't items left scattered throughout the car like an extra storage space or trash receptacle. He hadn't even found the normal junk stuffed in the armrest, only the charred edges of a few napkins.

The car was neat and orderly. Just like her home. And just like the office he suspected he'd find when he headed over to LSP later.

On a resigned sigh, he continued the review of the car, layer by layer. He'd need more time to take all the samples he wanted, but he did have enough to start the process. He needed to apprise his chief of what he'd discovered so far, so he'd kill two birds and drop the materials off at the lab himself. Maybe with some space and distance, and the idle time on the drive back to Austin, something would shake loose.

It was only ten minutes later, both he and Alex back in his SUV and headed for the highway, that it hit him. Whatever possible involvement Bellamy had in the situation unfolding at LSP, one thing was clear.

She'd been the target of a car bomb.

And since the perpetrator hadn't been successful, what would stop him from trying again?

Donovan skidded to a stop and took a hard spin on his steering wheel, whipping the car around before heading back into town and in the direction of Bellamy's house. Adrenaline lit him up like the Christmas lights on Main Street as he raced toward the small home.

Why had he let her walk out by herself? Worse, how had he been so blind to the needs of someone on his caseload?

The woman was at risk and in very clear danger.

And he'd been worried about a damn button and who she might be dating.

He pressed harder on the gas, bumping over the slightly uneven road that lead to her home. With yet another hard turn of the wheel, he spun onto her street. Relief punched through the adrenaline when he saw her in the distance, on her knees around the flower beds that surrounded the front porch, a hat on her head.

The scenario of smoke and fire that had accompanied him on the wild drive through town was nowhere in evidence. Instead, all he saw was a pretty woman on a cool Texas afternoon digging in her flower beds.

He'd never been more relieved.

Even as he couldn't shake the hard, insistent slam of his pulse that suggested he'd arrived just in time.

"Everything's fine, Dad. Really, it was nothing. It was an unfortunate accident, is all."

Jensen paced around his office, the faint voice of his father, Sutton Taylor, echoing from the speakerphone on his desk.

And everything *was* fine. Hadn't he been trying to tell the old man for half an hour already? Even confined to a bed, the old man could natter on and on.

"Bombs in cars? In our parking lot at headquarters?"

"An incident, nothing more."

"How can you say that, Jensen? It's an employee in danger. On our property."

In danger because I put her there. Voluntarily.

The retort was so close to the edge of his tongue Jensen nearly had to bite it, but held back. Gloating over his plans would get him nowhere and would prematurely tip his father off before he'd completed the work.

But he satisfied himself with a small smile, pleased that he'd found a way to get exactly what he wanted, all while pinning it on an unsuspecting victim.

Even better, no one would question the line of succession from Sutton to Jensen Taylor when the inevitable handoff of LSP finally came. He was the rightful heir to the Taylor family fortune and to Lone Star Pharmaceutical. His father might have enjoyed sowing every oat he had, but there was no way one of his bastards would get a single piece of what Jensen had worked for.

What he deserved.

"Dad, let the police do their job. Bellamy Reeves has been a loose cannon for some time."

"The sweet girl in finance?"

Jensen had to give his father credit—he did know his employees. Or maybe it was more that his father never forgot a pretty face. Whatever the reason, he'd pegged Jensen's scapegoat with surprising accuracy.

"She might have been sweet once but she's had a rough go these last few years. Her father was the one paralyzed in that accident several years ago."

"I knew Daniel-Justice Reeves, Jensen. I know what happened to the man."

Even with the sickness that had gripped him with increasing severity over the past few weeks, his father's withering voice was as clear as ever.

"Then you know he died a terrible death. Lingered there at the end way too long. That does something to a person, Dad. I don't know what I'd do if I was in the Reeves girl's position. If I lost you that way."

Sutton paused for a moment before continuing on in slightly quieter tones. "You need to help her. Find out who did this."

"Of course."

"And keep me posted. I'm not that far away."

"I know that. I know you can be back at any time." *Any freaking time*, Jensen thought. "I want you to focus on getting better. I'll figure out what's going on here and keep you updated."

"You can still come here for Christmas, you know," Sutton said, his voice quiet. "I'd like to see you."

The comment was almost sweet, for a man who'd never shown a large degree of fatherly care. *Nice time to try and mend fences, dear old Dad.*

But he said none of it. Instead, he forced that calm, capable tone into his voice, his focus on getting through the call. "I know I said I'd cover things through the holidays but that won't keep me from coming down to see you. You can count on me."

"All right. We'll talk tomorrow. Get Chief Thompson on this. I make sure that man has a rock-solid department with all the latest tools and tech for a reason. I want him taking care of this."

"Of course, Dad."

After a few more minutes of blustering, Jensen heard the voice of a nurse who'd puttered in to take Sutton's vitals and his father made excuses to hang up.

Jensen hit the end-call button on the speakerphone and stood there, staring out the window of his office at the view of the parking lot and the hill country beyond. He could still see the spot where Bellamy Reeves's car had been parked the day before, yellow police tape flying from a nearby tree. Even at this distance, a large black spot was visible on the ground from the remnants of the burned-out car.

His clueless little scapegoat.

She was the perfect choice. The absolutely perfect scapegoat for what he needed to do.

LSP would turn a shockingly enormous profit.

His father wouldn't be around to see any of it.

And one lonely, unlucky woman would take the fall before suffering a painful, lonely death.

How could he lose?

BELLAMY HEARD THE bark first, immediately followed by the solid poke of a squishy nose on her hip. She turned to see Alex playfully teasing her, his master standing about six feet away, hands on hips.

Her heart gave an involuntarily hitch at the sight he made. His thick, powerful shoulders were set off and backlit by the winter sun that rode low in the sky. The light breeze ruffled the edges of his hair, and his eyes were a warm, gooey chocolate-brownie brown as they stared down at her.

"We need to talk. Alex and I will check the grounds again and then we can discuss this morning."

Was that apology she saw reflected there? Remorse? Or neither, she quickly scolded herself as she dropped back on her rear and focused on Alex. Donovan was probably just here so he could scold her again.

"You checked the grounds this morning. Talk to me."

"It's important that I check things out."

"And it's important to me to talk to you."

To punctuate her point, she pulled off her gardening gloves and gave Alex a vigorous pat down, from the top of his head, down over his back and on toward the lower part of his spine as he wiggled in ecstasy. It didn't take much after that to push him to his side so she could give him the added joy of a belly rub.

"Careful. He might quit my team and join yours."

"Then I'd say he's one smart cookie." She patted Alex's chest before giving in and looking back up at Donovan. "I'm not sure I'd want to work for a suspicious brute, either."

"Suspicion comes with the territory. What did I do to get 'brute,' too?"

"You really don't know?"

"I'd rather hear it from your perspective."

Whatever she might suspect in his gaze, it was impossible to miss the sincerity, especially once she matched it to his voice. "You played the whole white knight routine this morning. Picking me up. Bringing me coffee. Even reassuring me it would be okay. And instead I walked into a firing squad."

"Chief Thompson wasn't quite that bad."

"He thinks I'm guilty. And so do you."

"Where'd you get that from?"

"The moment the two of you jumped all over those email printouts. I thought I had evidence of something horrible and all anyone who's looked at them has done is accuse me of doing something wrong. First Human Resources at LSP, right before they fired me. Then the two of you. I received that email and I have no idea who sent it or why."

Donovan dropped onto the grass beside her and reached for one of the garden gloves she'd dragged off to pet Alex. Toying with one finger, he twirled it in his hand and she tried her level best not to imagine him playing with her instead. Her hand inside that glove, her fingers trapped in his.

He would be warm, she imagined. His touch strong and capable. And how nice it would be to hang on in every one of those moments where she had no one to lean on except herself.

It'd be nice to hang on in all the other moments, too.

The thought was a surprise, the warmth that flooded her even more so.

Donovan Colton was the enemy.

Or at bare minimum a wary adversary, working at cross-purposes. There was no way she should even be entertaining thoughts of him in her life. Absolutely no reason at all to give them free rein.

"So talk to me, Bellamy."

"Why? So you can grill me again and make me feel like a common criminal?"

"No. Let's talk it through so we can try and find answers. Both the chief and I heard you today, though I'd like you to tell me again. But when I ask you questions, even the hard ones, don't assume it's because I don't believe you."

That sincerity was back, along with a subtle plea in his voice that tugged at her.

"Where do you want me to start?"

"At the beginning."

THE SUN BEAT down over his back as Donovan held his breath. He had driven over to Bellamy's like a madman, determined to get to her to make sure she was safe. Now that he was here, he'd done nothing but watch her, as smitten as Alex.

What was it about this woman?

She was beautiful, that was without question. Slim and lovely, she had a warmth about her that was hard to resist. It was funny, though, because he suspected if he asked her to describe herself she would outline a much harsher, tougher woman than the one who sat before him.

He imagined she saw herself as hard, maybe, because of the challenges she'd managed the past few years. But where she likely saw rough edges, he saw a diamond.

"What beginning?"

"Wherever you think this starts. You keep saying

the email you received yesterday. Do you think that's the right spot?"

"Isn't it?"

"It depends."

"On what?"

Did he tell her what he thought? He was a man who played his life close to the vest and police work had simply been a natural extension of that. He knew the roots of it all. More, he knew it was laughable how his worldview was steeped in every moment of his childhood. And from his continued embarrassment that he wasn't a true Colton.

He'd made the mistake of letting those feelings slip the year he turned fifteen, when he'd made an unsuccessful attempt to find his birth parents on the internet. Hays and Josephine and his siblings had spent the last sixteen years trying to change his mind.

Attempting to convince him he was as Colton as they come.

Oh, how he wished that were true. But he'd just gotten left in their barn one Christmas morning. Heck, he had better knowledge of Alex's lineage than his own.

"It depends on what, Donovan?"

Bellamy's intense focus and near breathless request caught him up short. This wasn't about him. Nor was it about whatever asinine issues he couldn't get over.

This was about her and her life and whatever lurked in the shadows, seemingly focused on her.

"Okay. Three things come to mind when I read that email. Either you inadvertently got information you shouldn't have or you've got information someone's using to embarrass LSP and were specifically targeted with it. Or you did it."

"I didn't!"

He raised his hands in a stop-don't-shoot gesture. "We're taking that one off the table, okay?"

"Okay." She nodded. "But even if we go with the first two, why do either? The company is a significant employer in this area. Their stock has risen year after year for over a decade. They've been on the leading edge in several health categories." Her gaze drifted to Alex as a small smile edged her lips. "We even have a robust veterinary medicine program in partnership with Texas A&M. I just don't see why the company would manipulate the drug supply or why someone with an intent to do ill would suggest they were. None of it rings true."

"Why not?"

Her eyes widened, the smile fading as her mouth dropped open. "Because it's illegal."

He fought his own smile at her innocence. Legality and illegality were lines far too many crossed easily and with impunity, nonplussed by the risk of consequences. For far too many, illegal activities were framed in one way only—don't get caught.

"Let's also table that it's illegal for now. Why don't either of those options ring true for you?"

She stilled, her eyes drifting over the flower beds as she thought over his question. Alex stared up at her, an enraptured expression on his face when her deep thoughts brought on additional belly rubs.

He seemed even more grateful when the belly rubs continued once she spoke again. "Sutton Taylor is our CEO. He's a good man and a great leader. He's not the sort to fix drug prices and throttle supply. It's just not possible."

Donovan wasn't quite ready to give any CEO such carte blanche for benevolence, but he wasn't ready to debunk her instincts there, either. "Okay. Anyone else?"

"I don't know. A disgruntled employee, maybe?"

"You have layoffs anytime in the recent past? It is the holidays. People out of work at Christmas have a lot of fair and well-aimed anger."

"The company hasn't had a single layoff since we brought a major Alzheimer's drug to market a decade ago."

"Okay. Who else? A landowner or a manufacturer? Maybe a government official? There are any number of worlds LSP plays in during the normal course of business. Lots of places an enemy could be lurking."

"Maybe. I guess." She shrugged at that. "I guess I could see it, but I simply don't have knowledge of all those areas. But—" She broke off, something alighting in her face. "Why would I get the email and be possibly framed if it were an area I had no knowledge of? I don't work in real estate or manufacturing. I don't even manage the finances for that area."

"What areas do you manage?"

"Drug trials, drug launches, go-to-market strategies and the relationships with our supply chain."

"There you go. So you are connected there."

"Connected to the degree that I know how it works. I know the players."

"So if someone were framing you, you'd be a person who others could believe might be involved."

"No!" Her hand stilled where it rested over Alex's fur. "Yes, maybe. I guess."

"That's where we need to focus."

"But who would do that to me?"

"We're going to find out."

A light breeze kicked up and with it, Alex shifted into motion. One moment he was flat on his back, tongue lolling in ecstasy, and the next he was on all fours, his nose buried in the ground as he took off through the grass.

"What's wrong?"

"I don't know." Donovan was up and after Alex, his partner's alert focus and intermittent barking all he needed to know.

Alex had found a scent.

Bellamy's property wasn't large and it didn't take Alex long to cover the ground, stopping before a small toolshed.

"What's wrong with him?" Bellamy nearly ran into his back before she stilled, her hand going to his shoulder to steady herself.

"He's fine. It's what he's found that's not. I need you to move back."

"You think he found something? In my shed?"

Since she hadn't moved, he did it himself, walking her back several steps to stand at the corner of the house.

"When was the last time you were in here?"

"An hour ago. I wanted to get my gardening equipment."

"And you didn't see anything odd or off?"

"No." She let out a long, low sigh. "I'm not sure I'd have seen much. I was angry and…well, I just slammed in and out of there without really looking at anything."

Donovan fought the shudder at what might have happened to her if she'd stepped the wrong place and instead focused on the matter at hand. "I need you to go to my car and get my equipment in the back. I need to make a call."

"For what?"

"Backup in Austin."

"Backup?" Her voice faded on that word, her eyes widening in dawning horror.

"If Alex's nose is right, and it always is, it looks like you've got a bomb in your shed. The last thing we need to do is set it off this close to the house."

Chapter Six

Bellamy fought the rising tide of panic that filled her stomach and crept up her throat.

A bomb?

In her shed?

She'd blithely walked past a few hours before.

A *bomb*.

One discovered by a sweet dog she'd been petting two minutes ago.

The anger and frustration she'd carried home from the police station vanished in full as she stared into the back of Donovan's SUV. Protective gear just as he described it filled the space, and she lifted out the thick jacket and headgear so he would be safe.

For her.

Shivers gripped her at the idea his life was in danger. She had a healthy enough self-image to know that she'd not asked for this or wished it on herself, but it didn't change the fact that Donovan was in danger on her behalf. Alex, too, for that matter.

"Bellamy! Did you find it?"

Her woolgathering at an end, she grabbed the gear and ran back to him. The materials were heavy and she was slightly winded by the time she got to him. "Here."

He took them easily, lifting them from her arms. "Go stand by the car, please."

"I can't leave you here."

"Go now. You can't be here. I'm protected and I know what I'm doing."

"I know, but—"

"I'll send Alex with you. He's good company and can stay with you until backup comes."

"Of course."

He ran a finger down her cheek in one long stroke. "I know what I'm doing. But it's easier to do it without worrying about you."

The movement was so unexpected and so very sweet she went with impulse. Without checking herself, she leaned in and pressed a quick, hard kiss to his lips. "Be careful."

The color of his already dark eyes deepened, drawing her in. "I will."

With quick instructions, Donovan ordered Alex to stay by her side. The black Lab trotted beside her, so close they nearly touched, all the way to the front yard. Sirens echoed in the distance and Bellamy braced herself for what came next.

More danger.

More suspicion.

And even more proof that someone was out to kill her.

DONOVAN HEARD THE sirens in the distance, mentally timing when his backup would arrive. He'd already calculated what might lay beyond the door and took some solace in the fact that she'd already entered and exited the shed once without detonating the device.

Dumb luck?

Or further proof they were dealing with an amateur?

The car bomb had been crude, the lapse in detonation time a pretty solid indicator they weren't dealing with an expert. But lack of skill didn't diminish the risk that the bastard would get lucky at some point.

There was the alternative—that someone was trying to scare Bellamy more than hurt her—but why? Even for experts, bombs were tricky things. If the goal was to frighten, there were a hell of a lot easier ways to accomplish that.

Which took him right back to an amateur, and the question that seemed to swirl at the center of all of this: What was going on at LSP?

The email had been quite clear. LSP was fixing prices and managing the supply of necessary flu vaccine. It seemed like an odd choice—surely there was more money to be made on other drugs. But flu was also ubiquitous. So many took the vaccine that keeping it out of circulation would incite panic.

And where there was panic and chaos, you had the right mix to put an object in demand.

Wasn't that the heart of all supply and demand? Make it seem irresistible and you made the product a must-have.

Only in this case, lives were at stake. The elderly and the infirm and small children all needed the vaccine to prevent an outbreak or to diminish the severity of one. How many people were ultimately protected by vaccines supplied by LSP?

Were there other pharmaceutical companies that could provide the needed supply if Lone Star couldn't?

Donovan didn't know enough about the specifics but

made a mental note to ask Bellamy later. If the supply chain really was damaged in all this, there had to be reasons it wasn't simply a matter of changing course and getting more vaccine from someone else.

His questions faded in full as the Whisperwood PD pulled up to Bellamy's house, the fire department in tow. Although they depended on Donovan's team in Austin as well as the K-9 unit for the majority of their bomb works, the local team was trained in basic detonation work and could support him as he walked through the proper procedures.

"What do you have there, Colton?" Chief Thompson hollered the request as he strode across Bellamy's yard.

"A hot one, if Alex's nose is any indication."

"Isn't his nose always an indication?"

"That's why you're here, Chief, while that hot sub you bought for lunch is getting cold on your desk."

"It's a cold sandwich today. It'll keep."

It was dopey banter, but it kept the situation moving forward until Archer could reach him. The man was already in protective gear that matched Donovan's, sans the helmet.

"What do you have?" The question was quiet, not meant for any potential bystanders or the small crowd gathered around Bellamy.

"Not sure yet. I don't think it's tied to the door, as Ms. Reeves went in and out about an hour ago, but I figured I'd wait to test that theory."

The chief nodded before asking a few more questions, then ordered his team forward to help set the scene. The fire department had already run their lines so they could quickly put out any potential blazes and an ambulance was on standby a bit farther down the road.

"It looks like Ms. Reeves is in a heap of trouble." The chief eyed the door before his gaze slipped back toward Bellamy. "A rather big heap."

"Sure seems that way." Donovan agreed.

"It also seems like a lot of trouble for someone to set this little scenario up all on their own."

"I was thinking along the same lines. Especially since she's so pale, it's a wonder she's not reflecting light right now." Donovan avoided turning back to look at that confused face for fear he'd lose his concentration. But even without looking, he knew she was scared.

And alone.

That thought had kept him company since his race across town and his discovery of the lone woman tending her garden. She didn't appear to have a support system, as she'd not mentioned anyone since he discovered her yesterday, huddled in the LSP parking lot staring at her car.

Was it really possible she was that alone?

He'd given her space the night before, even as his instincts kept suggesting she was into something they didn't fully understand.

But was it possible she'd been targeted specifically because she didn't have a support system? Or someone nearby paying close enough attention?

He wasn't exactly the poster child for familial happiness, but he could always count on his parents and siblings if he needed something.

But would you go to them?

The mental intrusion had him fumbling his hold on

his helmet and he fought to put it out of his mind as he righted his grip on the face cover.

This wasn't about him and he'd do well to keep his damn head in the damn game.

"So what do you say, Chief? Ready to open this one up?"

"I'd say. That sub's not going to eat itself."

Donovan hollered a few instructions to the assembled team, then reached for the shed door. Like a shiny present sitting under the Christmas tree, a small pressure cooker sat in the far corner of Bellamy's shed, easy to miss if you weren't paying attention.

Which she hadn't because she'd stomped in here, still mad at him and Archer.

A chill ran the length of his spine as he imagined what could have happened if the bomb was attached to the door, but forced it out of his mind. He could worry himself into a cold sweat later.

Right now he needed to get it handled.

The bomb was crude, reinforcing his impression that an amateur had made it. It had the same look and feel as the bombs that had littered news stories over the past decade, especially acts tied to homegrown terrorism. More than that, it was a device someone could easily discover how to build online and hastily put together, with the intention of doing localized harm.

Donovan moved closer, quickly cataloging the device before scanning the detonation mechanism. A small burner cell was wired to the device, its face dimly reflecting the fact that it was on and charged.

"You see the detonator?" Archer's voice was thick behind his mask but Donovan heard him and nodded.

"Yep. Burner cell."

"You know how to manage it?"

"Yep."

"Then let's get to work."

BELLAMY STOOD AT the end of her driveway, a crowd of EMS professionals surrounding her, and had never felt so alone or scared in all her life. Even with her parents—even at the very end—she hadn't felt this absolute sense of emptiness.

What had happened to her life?

Had she somehow brought this on herself? Pissed someone off at work so badly that they'd decided to make her pay?

Because whatever this was, it was highly personal. First her car and then her home. Which meant whoever was doing this knew what she drove and where she lived.

Unbidden, an image of Sally Borne's hard face popped into her mind. HR would have access to her personnel files, including her home address. They also knew her license plate because it was needed as part of the documentation to receive a badge to the LSP property.

Alex leaned against her leg, the heavy weight of his body a reassuring comfort as she stood there, puzzling through all the implications. She laid a hand on this head and stroked the soft fur that grew even softer where it ran down the backs of his ears. He seemed to understand what she needed, pressing his head into her hand when she stilled, insisting she keep up with the soothing, steady strokes.

The dog was a marvel. She'd always loved pets but had never found time to own one. In the years before her father's accident she'd been busy with work and never felt she could give an animal the proper attention. And after, once there were pills and wheelchairs and a constant focus on keeping him well, it didn't seem like the right time.

Perhaps that had been more shortsighted than she realized. Her father would have responded well to a pet, a gentle friend to keep him company each day. And for herself, it would be nice to have a companion to come home to now. A warm, furry body who was happy to see her.

Maybe if she had a dog they'd have warned her of whatever was lurking around the house and putting bombs in her shed.

Alex laid his head against her thigh and let out a soft sigh. He was a funny creature, she thought as she took comfort in his large body, with a fierce devotion and gentle personality. It was easy to see what he was thinking and she had no doubt he *was* thinking. It might be veiled through the lens of canine understanding, but there was something going on behind those dark brown eyes.

More, there was a fierce protection there that promised the dog knew his purpose in life and would carry it out without fail.

Purpose.

Understanding settled over her, a soothing balm in the midst of the chaos that surrounded her. She'd had purpose once. A focus on the life that stretched before her and the goals she'd set for herself.

Somewhere along the way, she'd lost that. Yes, her parents had needed care and attention. At times, that had taken precedence over other choices in her life.

But she'd been solely responsible for losing her sense of self. For allowing what was happening around her to take possession of her dreams instead of keeping them firmly in her sights.

Whatever her future held or however long she had, it was time to make a change.

Alex let out a large bark at her side, a funny punctuation mark to the definitiveness of her thoughts. But it was the quivering beneath her hand and the immediate thump of his tail that had her smiling just as Donovan came around the corner of the house.

He held a small silver bowl in his hands that took shape as he got closer. A pressure cooker? She had one herself, buried in the back of the cabinet on the rare occasions she decided to cook rice for a week of meals. What was one doing in her shed?

It was only as she saw the wires dangling from beneath his gloved hands that she understood. That was the bomb. Positioned in her shed and ready to cause irreparable damage.

Ready to kill her.

A wave of nausea flooded her stomach as she took in the innocuous kitchen appliance turned into a device that could end her life.

With a gentle push, she urged Alex forward. "Go see him." The dog seemed to waver only a moment before she patted his back and pressed him forward. "Go!"

He ran to Donovan, his focus on the device in his partner's hands. Donovan bent over, allowing the dog to sniff the contents, praising him for his understanding of the threat. His tail wagged at the praise, and again, Bellamy was amazed at all the animal communicated without words.

Where his tail had thumped with the excitement of seeing his master, now it wagged with the determined understanding of the job they did and the risk to the people around them.

The dog *knew*. He understood on a base level that was fascinating to watch.

But it was the body language of his master that had Bellamy taking a step back. Even encased in the heavy protection gear, she could see the purpose and determination as he walked across her yard. He innately understood the danger in the device in his hands—more, he knew the danger it posed to her—and with that knowledge he carried the responsibility for fixing it.

SALLY BORNE SCANNED the email on her phone before tossing the device onto her desk. "Merry freaking Christmas to me."

What had she gotten herself into? Worse, what sort of ridiculous sweet nothings had Jensen Taylor managed to put into her ear that had made her think any of this was a good idea?

She was smarter than this. Had *always* been smarter than this.

So why had she listened to the little slimeball?

Especially since it had become increasingly obvious his father was neither on the verge of turning over the company nor getting ready to enter into his dotage. Hell, she'd have been better off seducing Sutton Taylor. If she was fifteen years younger, she might have tried, but those rheumy old eyes could still pick out a stacked twenty-five-year old at fifty yards. She had a complaint file from several sales reps in her top drawer to prove it.

Unable to hold back the sneer, she thought of the last one who'd pranced in and complained about Sutton's less-than-subtle attentions.

Ridiculous.

When you had assets, you used them. Those same reps weren't above using a little T & A when they visited doctors, selling in LSP's latest offerings. You'd think they'd be more appreciative when the head of the company appreciated the same thing they were flaunting to fill their pockets.

Brushing it off, she picked up her phone and read the email from the police one more time. The friendships she'd cultivated at the Whisperwood PD had paid off and the update on Bellamy Reeves's visit to the station that morning was detailed and thorough. The little bitch had a copy of the email and had freely handed it off to the chief.

Sally reread the last line of the message, heartened that the ploy might end up working in their favor. The lack of sender and the strange nature of the missive had put some doubt in the chief's mind, suggesting that poor little Bellamy Reeves had gone around the bend and was setting this all up for her own benefit as a way to defraud and manipulate the company.

Curious, Sally sat down and pulled out the Reeves file. She flipped through the personnel records, the praise for Bellamy clear on every review and evaluation as well as the input sheets tied to her past promotions.

The woman had a stellar reputation. She was well liked, kept to herself and avoided causing any drama at work. A model employee.

Of course, there was the matter of her family. A loss like that was something that changed a person. It erupted in the middle of life, taking everything you once knew and turning it upside down.

There was power in that. A story she could weave, tightening the threads until they were impossible to unravel.

Shifting to her laptop, Sally began her reply to the Whisperwood PD. No reason not to seed a bit more doubt about poor, sad Bellamy Reeves, preparing to enter the holiday season all alone.

DONOVAN STRIPPED OFF the protective gear and laid it in the back of his SUV. He'd already turned the evidence over to Archer, tagging it with the necessary markers from his side and calling it in to his own chief to keep the man updated. He'd been given the order to stay in Whisperwood until this was handled, the focus on Lone Star Pharmaceutical ensuring his chief didn't want any blowback from the investigation.

If he hadn't been given the go-ahead to stay, he'd have asked anyway, the risks to Bellamy too concerning to leave her alone. But now that he was here, he needed to figure out how to get her to agree to his plan.

Not only was he not going to leave her alone, but he and Alex would stay to guard her. He'd nearly made up his mind on the drive over, but now it was a done deal, especially when it was more than obvious that whoever had targeted her wasn't above escalating their tactics to her home.

Once again, the crudeness of the bomb struck him as he nestled his gear into its proper place. A pressure cooker bomb? It was far from elegant and the fact that they'd been in the news as incendiary devices gave further credence to an amateur picking up on something and running with it. Easy to purchase and easy to build, it made the perfect device for limited range, deliberate hits.

He and his fellow K-9 team members had seen an increase in the devices and the lunatics who thought a homemade bomb made a nice, clean, easy way to deal with a problem. It was a coward's way to kill, far removed from the point of impact, the perpetrator safe at a distance.

And it was easy because no one had to stick around and face the damage.

Just like your mother, dropping you off in the Colton barn, abandoned on Christmas morning.

His hand shook as he laid his headgear on top of his flak suit, the connection between his own birth and a bomb was one that hit way too close to home. Yet even as he rejected the maudlin thoughts, something about them stuck.

It was easy to do the wrong thing when you didn't have to stick around and face the consequences.

"Donovan? Are you all right?"

He turned to see Bellamy, her hands still against her sides as she took him in. The moment struck him, her slender form clad in a simple T-shirt and yoga pants backlit by the afternoon sun. That same breeze that had tipped Alex off to the bomb in the shed whispered around them once more, a bit cooler as the afternoon edged toward evening, a bit wilder as it blew her hair against her face.

"I'm good."

"How do you do that? You walked in, not knowing what you were going to find."

"It's part of the job description."

Dear Reader,

Since you are a lover of our books, your opinions are important to us... and so is your time.

That's why we made sure your **"FAST FIVE" READER SURVEY** can be completed in just a few minutes. Your answers to the five questions will help us remain at the forefront of women's fiction.

And, as a thank-you for participating, we'd like to send you **4 FREE THANK-YOU GIFTS!**

Enjoy your gifts with our appreciation,

Pam Powers

To get your
4 FREE THANK-YOU GIFTS:

✳ Quickly complete the "Fast Five" Reader Survey
and return the insert.

"FAST FIVE" READER SURVEY

1 Do you sometimes read a book a second or third time? ○ Yes ○ No

2 Do you often choose reading over other forms of entertainment such as television? ○ Yes ○ No

3 When you were a child, did someone regularly read aloud to you? ○ Yes ○ No

4 Do you sometimes take a book with you when you travel outside the home? ○ Yes ○ No

5 In addition to books, do you regularly read newspapers and magazines? ○ Yes ○ No

YES! I have completed the above Reader Survey. Please send me my 4 FREE GIFTS (gifts worth over $20 retail). I understand that I am under no obligation to buy anything, as explained on the back of this card.

❏ I prefer the regular-print edition
182/382 HDL GMVS

❏ I prefer the larger-print edition
199/399 HDL GMVS

FIRST NAME	LAST NAME

ADDRESS

APT.#	CITY

STATE/PROV.	ZIP/POSTAL CODE

READER SERVICE—Here's how it works:

Accepting your 2 free Harlequin Intrigue® books and 2 free gifts (gifts valued at approximately $10.00 retail) places you under no obligation to buy anything. You may keep the books and gifts and return the shipping statement marked "cancel." If you do not cancel, about a month later we'll send you 6 additional books and bill you just $4.99 each for the regular-print edition or $5.74 each for the larger-print edition in the U.S. or $5.74 each for the regular-print edition or $6.49 each for the larger-print edition in Canada. That is a savings of at least 12% off the cover price. It's quite a bargain! Shipping and handling is just 50¢ per book in the U.S. and 75¢ per book in Canada*. You may cancel at any time, but if you choose to continue, every month we'll send you 6 more books, which you may either purchase at the discount price plus shipping and handling or return to us and cancel your subscription. *Terms and prices subject to change without notice. Prices do not include applicable taxes. Sales tax applicable in N.Y. Canadian residents will be charged applicable taxes. Offer not valid in Quebec. Books received may not be as shown. All orders subject to approval. Credit or debit balances in a customer's account(s) may be offset by any other outstanding balance owed by or to the customer. Please allow 4 to 6 weeks for delivery. Offer available while quantities last.

▼ If offer card is missing write to: Reader Service, P.O. Box 1867, Buffalo, NY 14240-8531 or visit www.ReaderService.com ▼

BUSINESS REPLY MAIL
FIRST-CLASS MAIL   PERMIT NO. 717   BUFFALO, NY

POSTAGE WILL BE PAID BY ADDRESSEE

READER SERVICE
PO BOX 1341
BUFFALO NY 14240-8571

NO POSTAGE
NECESSARY
IF MAILED
IN THE
UNITED STATES

"Yes, but it's—" She broke off, her beautiful mouth dropping down into a frown. "But you didn't know what was behind the door."

"Believe it or not, you inadvertently helped there."

"How?"

"While it gives me the chills to say this, you'd already gone through the door. And even though that wasn't a foolproof method, it did indicate the bomb wasn't pressure sensitive to the opening of the door."

She seemed to shrink in on herself at that and he reached out to take a hand, squeezing the slim fingers. "Thanks for the assist. Try not to do that again, please."

"Okay."

Her hand was cold in his and it dragged at him, twisting him up even further about the fact that something could have happened to her. Without checking the impulse, he tugged on her hand, pulling her forward so she was flush against him. In one long move, he seated himself on the back bumper of the SUV, pulling her between his legs as he dragged her mouth down to his.

His seated position gave her the height advantage, but he had the benefit of surprise. When she'd kissed him in front of the shed earlier, she'd surprised him with the power of the simple gesture.

Something inside of him—something hungry and raw and the slightest bit scared—wanted to feel that again. Wanted to feel the heat and the life and the sheer beauty of her pressed against him.

It was with a hunger for all those things and something even more—something distinctly Bellamy—that had his tongue pressing into her mouth, satisfied as she granted him ready access. If this kiss had surprised her, she'd quickly caught up, her tongue meeting his stroke for luscious stroke.

And then she turned the tables on him, her hands wrapping around his shoulders and neck, her fingers lingering at the base of his neck. What had been cool to the touch heated quickly, those exploring fingers also pressing his head to hers, fusing their mouths as each plundered the other.

His hands moved over her hips, tracing the length of her tantalizing curves as the kiss continued to spin out, a sensual web of feeling. It was erotic, the meeting of tongues, the light winter breeze over their skin and the simple touch of their hands on each other.

Donovan knew he should pull away. Knew even better that this was not only ill-advised, but a massive conflict of interest.

Yet, even with the sense of duty that drummed beneath his skin, he couldn't walk away. Couldn't tear himself back or pull away from something so lovely and tantalizing and *real*.

It was the last that gripped him in tight fists.

She was real. Yes, she was beautiful and sensual and appealing as a woman, but she was so much more. He respected her bravery and her determination. Even more, he valued her belief in her truth and her refusal to back down or be cowed by what was happening around her.

"Donovan." Her whisper against his mouth broke the kiss and he tried to nip her bottom lip once more, unwilling to end the sweetly sensual moment.

"Donovan." She whispered it again, even as her lips curved into a smile.

"What?"

"The chief is still here."

He surfaced quickly at that news, combined with Archer's hard cough as Bellamy slipped out of his arms and moved to stand a few feet away from the SUV.

"Archer."

"Donovan."

Donovan knew the man's blue eyes were twinkling, even though he couldn't see them behind the dark lenses of his sunglasses.

"I think we're wrapped up here," Archer said.

"I thought we already were."

"I'm going to need another statement, but seeing as how I was here as it all unfolded, I think I can write up the majority of what we need for the report. Perhaps you could escort Ms. Reeves to the station tomorrow to provide any needed details."

"That will be fine," Bellamy quickly added from where she stood beside Alex.

Archer obviously sensed his presence was no longer welcome and he made a hasty retreat, a tip of his hat before he took off.

A light flush covered Bellamy's face before following a lovely path down her neck and over her collarbone. "He certainly got here quick."

"Shame he couldn't leave as quickly." Donovan's hands still itched and he heard the hoarse, husky notes in his voice. He'd forgotten where he was. Utterly and completely, as he'd fallen into that kiss.

And Chief Thompson had known it, his eyes twinkling as he'd said his goodbyes.

Twinkling, for Pete's sake.

Donovan glanced at Alex, unsurprised to see a large

grin painting his furry face as he panted into the breeze beside Bellamy.

The entire situation would have been funny if he hadn't diffused a bomb in Bellamy's shed. A point only reinforced by the high-pitched cry of a woman who peeled to a stop in front of the driveway, running toward Bellamy as the car still idled in her wake.

"Are you okay? I just heard the news." The woman was attractive, a tall, thin blonde dressed in needle-sharp heels, elegant black slacks and a silk blouse that likely would cost him a week's salary. It was all set off by flashy jewelry that seemed to drip from her, including a large diamond that lay against her collarbone.

Donovan gave the woman credit—she moved in the heels—and watched as she flung her arms around Bellamy's shoulders, pulling her close. He wouldn't have believed it if he wasn't standing there watching, but Bellamy stiffened up so much she could have been a poker standing beside the small fireplace in her living room.

But it was the ice that dripped from her tone that truly caught him off guard.

"Hi, Maggie. What are you doing here?"

The woman pulled back, her shoulders slumping at the greeting. "I'm your sister. Of course I came. What I don't understand is why you didn't call me right away."

"Because I'm fine."

Fine?

The diffused bomb even now being driven to the Whisperwood police station suggested otherwise, but it was the distinct sense of unease and anger telegraphing from Bellamy's rigid frame that truly pulled him up short.

What was going on here?

And what sort of issue could Bellamy Reeves possibly have with her sister?

Chapter Seven

"I'm fine, Maggie. Really. How many times do I have to say it?"

Bellamy heard the coarse, stilted words that spilled from her lips and wanted to pull them back. She wished that she could find a way to get past the anger and the confusion that marked her relationship with her sister.

It hadn't always been like this. No one had been happier to have a baby sister than her. She'd welcomed sweet little Maggie along with her parents and the two of them had been inseparable as kids, even with a five-year age difference.

Maggie had always seemed so fragile and waifish, and Bellamy had developed a mix of protectiveness and encouragement for her sister that she gave to no one else. That gentle, fragile nature had changed over the years and by the time Bellamy graduated from high school, Maggie was getting ready to enter, already the belle of Whisperwood. People spoke of her beauty and their parents doted on her, willing to give their precious baby anything she wanted.

The sweet little soul Bellamy had cared for and protected suddenly didn't need her any longer and it had hurt to realize, as she went off to college, that she wasn't the center of her sister's world anymore.

It had taken several years and making of new friends with fresh perspectives while she was away at school for Bellamy to realize her sister didn't need a second mother, but a friend. But by the time she'd returned to Whisperwood, Maggie's life had shifted in new directions, including spending time with the popular crowd, riding around town in her convertible and winning the heart of half the boys in school.

She'd been happy for Maggie, even if she was forced to accept that her own life had turned out very differently. The job at LSP had provided another fresh perspective and after immersing herself in work and a new group of friends and colleagues, the distance with Maggie didn't seem to matter so much.

Or maybe she'd just stopped caring any longer if it hurt.

She'd had a life and a job she loved and a future to look forward to. Life was good and if she didn't have a strong relationship with her sister, then it was something she'd live with.

"Bellamy, did you hear me? What is going on around here? First I hear about a bomb that blows up your car and now I hear there's one in the shed, too?" Maggie settled three glasses of iced tea on the small drop leaf table Bellamy kept in the corner of her kitchen, handing one over. "And hurry up and tell me before the always attractive Donovan Colton comes back inside. Goodness, I remember him from high school. He was a year ahead of me but what a looker."

Something in the casual assessment of Donovan spiked her ire once more and Bellamy fought to hold her tongue. Whatever her relationship with Maggie, spitting at her like a she-cat—a *jealous* she-cat—wasn't the way to handle things.

"He's part of the K-9 team out of Austin. He's been assigned to my case."

"He's done well for himself. I'd heard he was getting into K-9 a few years after joining the Austin PD."

"How'd you hear that?"

Maggie shrugged, her perfect blond hair rising and falling with the motion. "The Coltons are always the subject of local gossip. People talk, Bell, you know that."

"Is that all people in this town are to you? Gossip? Is that why you rushed over here? So you'd be in the know."

Maggie's glass stopped halfway to her lips, her mouth drawing down in a frown. Carefully, she set the glass back on the table before shifting her cool blue gaze fully to Bellamy's. "I realize you and I have had our differences, but I don't understand how you could think I don't care about you."

"You've never seemed all that interested in taking part in my life."

"You shut me out! Just because I saw how we should be caring for Mom and Dad differently than you did, doesn't mean I'm some horrible person."

"You wanted to put them in a home."

"No, I wanted them to get the proper care they deserved while taking the burden off of you."

"They're my parents. I did it willingly."

"And are now playing the martyr because you did."

That unpleasant rebuttal settled in the middle of the

table between them, an oozing pile of resentment and anger that only seemed to grow bigger and more acidic.

How was it that things had gone so badly between them? They'd barely spent ten minutes with each other and were already fighting. Yet even as it bothered her, she couldn't fully kill the resentment and the anger.

"Why are you really here? I can't imagine James would be happy with you putting yourself in danger by being so close to a crime scene."

"James doesn't much care what I do." Maggie ran a hand over the cold condensation on her glass, her cornflower blue gaze averted. "Our divorce will be final in early January. Just after New Year's Day, as a matter of fact."

"Your what?"

The resentment and anger grew smaller and faded in the face of Maggie's news, before vanishing away as Bellamy moved around the table to take Maggie's hand. "When did this happen?"

"Earlier this year."

"But why? How? I thought you were so happy being married."

"We were married. Happiness wasn't a big part of it. A situation that got worse when he informed me he wasn't interested in having children."

"Oh."

She'd not been a part of her sister's life for some time, but the finality of that statement left its sting, chunking away a bit more of her years-old anger. "I'm sorry, Maggie. Really sorry."

"It's fine. We've said a lot of horrible things to each other and now we've just become numb. The New Year can't get here fast enough."

Bellamy wanted to say more—felt she *should* say more—but had no right. Whatever frustrations she might have over Maggie's behavior the past several years, she wouldn't have wished the dissolution of her marriage on her.

Neither would she ever have suspected there was anything wrong in the first place. James Corgan came from one of the wealthiest families in the state and had always seemed smitten with Maggie. Their marriage had happened quickly, but Bellamy had always assumed it was a love match.

Was she wrong about that? Or had things simply gone wrong, the same way her relationship with Maggie had changed into something neither of them recognized any longer?

"I guess we've both been keeping secrets."

"I'm not keeping secrets."

"Oh no?" Maggie raised a lone, perfect eyebrow. "Then what's going on that has you the target of bombings?"

"I have no idea."

"Come on, Bell. This is real life, not TV. People don't just walk out to their car after work and nearly get blown up."

"I'm well aware of that. It still doesn't mean I have a clue to what's going on."

The lie tripped right on out, practically skipping around the room. For the first time in a long time, she wanted to open up to Maggie—wanted to tell her about the email she'd received—but she had no idea how. If she said something, would she put Maggie in danger, too?

And if she told her, she would also have to admit

that she was out of work. She still hadn't figured out how she was going to handle the taxes on the house her parents had left her or what she was going to do about getting a new car. She had a little bit saved, but nothing that was going to see her without a job indefinitely.

Especially if Sally Borne made good on her threat to blackball her from getting another.

"This is ridiculous." Maggie drummed one painted fingernail on the table. "Surely you have to know something. Or we can ask around and find someone who might know what this is about."

"I'm not making my personal life gossip fodder for the town."

"But if someone can help you…"

"No. I will handle this and deal with it myself."

"Just like you always do."

Whatever subtle truce they'd arrived at vanished completely as Bellamy got to her full height. "Yes, Maggie. Just like I always do. I can handle myself and whatever comes my way. I've been doing it for years."

The door to the kitchen opened at that moment, Donovan and Alex barreling into the room in a rush of feet and paws. The echo of Bellamy's retort still hovered but even if Donovan had missed the words, there was no way he missed her standing up, hands fisted at her sides.

"Everything okay?"

"Fine. Absolutely fine." Bellamy stepped away from her seat, extending a hand to Donovan and gesturing him to sit in her place. "Let me just get some fresh water for Alex."

The ploy was either enough to divert attention or Donovan was simply too polite to say otherwise, but he took the offered seat as Maggie thrust his glass of iced tea on him while Bellamy busied herself with some water for Alex.

The awkwardness of the moment was quickly covered up with Maggie's questions, her voice a sensual purr now that she was in the presence of an attractive man. As she listened, settling a large bowl of water on the floor, Bellamy felt herself closing up even further.

It didn't matter how badly she wished things were different with her sister; it wasn't possible.

And just like the loss of her parents, she was simply going to have to find a way to accept it.

DONOVAN PLACED HIS empty glass of iced tea back on the kitchen table and counted off the number of minutes until he could make a polite excuse and leave the room once more. If he'd known what he was walking into, he'd have found a way to stay outside with Alex a bit longer.

But they'd already done two perimeter sweeps of Bellamy's small property line and found nothing. Nor had they found anything else inside the shed, even after Donovan ran Alex through the drill a second and third time. He'd finally given in and gotten a fresh treat out of the car, sorry that he'd put Alex through such rigor over an obviously clean site.

Which was one more proof point that he was too far around the bend over Bellamy Reeves. He trusted Alex implicitly. The dog was well trained and had never let him down. That wasn't about to change.

What he now needed to figure out was how he was going to get Bellamy to let him stay. There was no way he was heading back to Austin and leaving her alone.

He briefly toyed with the idea of leaving her at his parents' home. He would consider it if things went truly sideways, but wasn't quite ready to give in and bring his family into this mess.

Which left him and Alex as her newest houseguests.

He'd met the woman who'd arrived earlier, remembering her after the basic introductions. Maggie Reeves had been a year behind him in high school but he still recalled her reputation as one of the most popular kids. Funny how it hadn't mattered to him then and mattered even less now.

Yet somehow, in looking at Bellamy's sister, he sensed it was deeply important to how she saw herself.

"It's been a long time since I've seen you," Maggie said, her smile broad.

"High school, probably." Donovan nodded after taking a sip of his iced tea. "I haven't spent much time in Whisperwood since then."

"What brings you here now?"

"I'm part of the APD's K-9 unit. We support the surrounding communities in addition to Austin and I'm here to help the chief."

"On Bellamy's case?"

"Among others."

Donovan heard the genuine interest in Maggie's voice, but couldn't shake the underlying tension that hovered in the kitchen. He was the last person to criticize family dynamics, but there was a stiffness to Maggie and Bellamy's relationship that struck him as sad.

Not your business, Colton.

And it wasn't. But knowing what Bellamy had been through in the past few days, he couldn't understand why she wouldn't lean on her sister.

"What you do must be fascinating. Law enforcement. And working with your sweet dog, too."

Maggie kept her distance from Alex, but Donovan had seen how her gaze kept darting to the large form currently slurping water in the corner of the small kitchen. Even that was curious. Bellamy had warmed to Alex immediately, but Maggie kept looking at him as if he were going to attack her at any moment.

"Alex is my full partner. We work together to find and diffuse bombs as well as missing persons and drugs."

"Wow." Her gaze shifted to the dog once again, but her tension seemed to ebb ever so slightly. "He can do all that?"

"He's pretty amazing. His nose can find far more than we can ever understand. And his training ensures he knows how to tell me what he's found."

Jiggling the ice cubes in his glass, Donovan glanced over at his partner, now seated on his haunches with his tongue lolling. "We're going to leave you two alone. Alex and I have a few more things we need to do outside."

Before anyone could protest, Donovan made his escape, a quick nod all the dog needed to follow along. They weren't outside more than ten minutes when Maggie found her way to the back of his SUV. Donovan finished reordering his gear and turned at her quiet greeting.

"Hello, Ms. Reeves."

"It's Corgan. Maggie Corgan. For at least a little while longer." She muttered that last piece, even as a bright smile remained firmly on her face.

"Of course. What can I do for you?"

"Bell and I have a tough relationship. We haven't agreed on a lot of things for a long time and it's chipped away at what we used to have."

While he couldn't deny his loyalty to Bellamy, something in Maggie's words tugged at him. He knew what it was to have a distance between him and his loved ones. More, he knew what it was to want to close that distance but have no idea where to start.

"I love my sister," Maggie continued. "I care for her very much and I hate to think that she's in danger. Please take care of her. And please keep me posted if there's anything I can do."

"This is an active investigation but I'll do my best."

"Thanks. I guess that's all I can ask."

He watched her walk away, her physical look at odds with what he sensed lay beneath the surface. Maggie Corgan was a beautiful woman. Her hair was perfect, as were her body, her clothes, her car and her jewelry.

Yet beneath it all he sensed a woman who had very little.

As Maggie started her car and drove off, Donovan wondered if Bellamy understood that at all.

BELLAMY PUTTERED AROUND the kitchen, at odds with herself. Donovan and Alex were still outside—his SUV was visible in the driveway—but she didn't want to go out to see what they were doing. Maggie's visit had hit hard and she was still raw over the way they'd left things.

Her sister's news was unsettling, as well. It was the holidays and here Maggie was anticipating a divorce in the next few weeks. A small voice whispered that she should have invited her to spend the holidays together but she'd ignored it. And allowed the years-old anger and pain to prevent her from saying anything.

Wherever she'd once expected to be in life, thirty-five and alone, with no relationship with her sister, was so not it.

Which meant she needed to do something.

She retrieved the empty glasses from the kitchen table and washed them all in the sink, and was drying the last one when Donovan and Alex returned to the kitchen.

"We've swept your yard and shed three times and haven't found anything. You're clean."

Clean? Just like the glasses, only instead of washing out a bit of iced tea, he was hunting for bombs. Items designed to maim and kill. On a hard swallow, Bellamy nodded. "Thank you."

"I'd like to discuss what's going to happen next."

"Of course."

"You can't stay here. Not by yourself."

"Where do you think I'm going to go?"

"Your sister's would be a place to start."

Whatever ideas she had about making things better with Maggie, dragging her into this mess wasn't one of them. Bellamy pushed back from the counter and crossed the kitchen to face Donovan. "Absolutely not."

"She cares for you. And she's worried."

The thick lines of his body projected capable strength and something inside of Bellamy melted. How easy would it be to just move in, wrap her arms around him and sink in? The imprint of his lips lingered on hers, the heady sensation of their kiss still in the forefront of her mind.

But much as she wanted to talk to him and tell him

how she felt about her relationship with Maggie and all that she desperately wished she could make right, it wasn't his problem.

None of this was his problem.

And a few kisses couldn't change that.

"I'm not bringing her into this." Bellamy said.

"But we can put protection on you both. Can make sure no one harms either of you."

"I'm staying in my house. That's non-negotiable."

"You can't stay here alone. That's why Alex and I are moving in until this is handled."

"You can't move in." The words came out on a squeak, even as a sly sense of delight curled beneath her skin.

"Since you seem to feel similar about going to your sister's, it's the only way."

Bellamy ignored how neatly Donovan made his argument and searched for some way to push back. "But this is my house. And you're assigned to my case. You can't live here."

"This is Whisperwood. The town is small and I'm from here. The department is well staffed but they don't need to put someone out here full-time. And I can work from here as well as Austin. On the few times I need to head into the city you can come with me."

"You can't upend my life this way."

Donovan glanced down at Alex, his smile broad as he placed a hand on the dog's head. "We just did."

THE UPENDING OF her life began immediately, and with surprising regularity. True to his promise, Donovan and Alex kept close watch on her and their days together had taken on an odd sort of routine.

Four days into life with her new roommates, Bellamy found herself once again heading down I-35 with Donovan and Alex, straight into Austin. The afternoon traffic was thick, with cars bumper-to-bumper as they approached downtown.

"This is ridiculous."

"No more ridiculous than a woman who's fighting off bomb threats to her life."

"I meant the traffic," Bellamy said. "I sort of thought the rest of it all had moved into the realm of the absurd."

His grin was broad as he glanced over at her. "Consider it an absurdity I'm determined to end."

She was grateful for that, the quick confidence that he could fix things going a long way toward soothing the nerves that refused to abate. She'd forget about the situation at LSP and her car and her shed for a few moments, and then it would all come streaming back, like a film on constant replay.

She wanted to believe it was over—a temporary madness that had descended in her life and vanished just as quickly—but the presence of man and dog suggested otherwise.

As did the unshakable feeling that things weren't over, no matter how badly she wanted them to be.

"You really believe you can stop whatever's going on?"

"Of course. That's my job. That, and keeping you safe in the process."

"Isn't that the chief's job?"

"We work together. Archer Thompson's a good man. If it's on his caseload, he's committed to handling things."

"For the biggest employer in Whisperwood. Isn't that a conflict?"

The easy smile vanished. "You always go around accusing the police of being in people's pockets?"

"I'm not—" She broke off, aware that was exactly what she was doing. "No, I'm not trying to suggest that. But I do know that much of his funding comes from the fact that LSP is such a huge business in Whisperwood. The tax contribution alone is significant. It can't be easy for the chief to have to investigate them."

"There's nothing easy about his job. Doesn't mean he can't handle it."

The quiet stretched out between them once more and Bellamy was forced to look at her behavior through Donovan's eyes. What must he see when he looked at her? A lonely woman, living in a small house all by herself. No obvious ties to anyone to speak of, made more evident by what he'd observed between her and Maggie. And now she was going around accusing the Whisperwood police of corruption.

The thought had whispered through her mind more than once over the past few days, but now that it had taken root, something had the words spilling from her lips.

"I wasn't always like this."

"Like what?"

"Suspicious and unkind."

"Is that how you see yourself?" Donovan kept his eyes firmly on the traffic but it took no less power out of his question.

"Some days. Others I feel like I'm drifting through life on autopilot, not sure how I got there."

"You suffered a big loss. You're entitled to grieve."

"Am I? Or has it become a convenient excuse to stop living?"

SOMETHING IN BELLAMY'S words tugged at Donovan. He wouldn't have called her unkind—hadn't even considered her through that lens—but he did see the suspicion and the anger.

And the fear.

How did a person deal with that, day in and day out? Yes, the bomb threats were new, but dealing with ill and infirm parents, then losing them, had been a part of her life for far longer. That sort of pressure would change anyone.

"I'm the last person qualified to answer that question."

"Why?"

"I've lived on autopilot myself for an awfully long time. Gets to a point where you stop noticing it anymore."

He hadn't expected to say that much and the words left a bitter aftertaste on his lips.

Bellamy didn't immediately respond. It was only when he felt the light touch on his hand, where it lay over the center armrest, that she spoke. "What are you running from?"

"The same thing I've been running from my entire life. I'm not a Colton and my family refuses to see that."

"What do you mean, you're not a Colton?"

"I'm not. I was left in the Colton stables Christmas morning thirty-one years ago. Hays and Josephine took me in but I'm not their son."

"Of course you are. They're your family. Adoption or biology doesn't change that."

Her ready defense was sweet but Donovan had lived a lifetime feeling like an imposter. A poser. The truth haunted him and only grew worse this time of year.

"It changes everything. I'm not one of them, no matter how much they want to believe otherwise."

"Biology doesn't dictate your relationships. Look at Maggie and me. We're sisters and we can't seem to find common ground. What matters is the relationships you have. The love you have for each other. The family you make."

"You don't love your sister?"

"Of course I love her."

The emphatic response gave him heart that there was a path for Bellamy to move forward with her sister, but the dichotomy of their familial situations wasn't lost on him.

"So you have a family you can't seem to reconcile with, and I have a family who wants me in it and I keep walking away. Is that it?"

"When you put it like that, I suppose so," she agreed.

"Family's hard. It's messy and emotional. That's why I love animals so much. They take you just the way you are."

"From what you've said, the Coltons took you just the way you were. You're the one who doesn't want to accept that."

Bellamy's words lingered long after they cleared Austin traffic and entered downtown. Donovan didn't want to believe them—didn't want to accept that he was the one who'd rejected his family's love—but the lingering guilt that had accompanied him since he was young glommed on to her statement.

And way down deep inside, he knew she was right.

Chapter Eight

The K-9 training center was quiet for midafternoon, but Donovan hardly noticed it as he unclipped Alex's leash and let him bound off into the large grassy area they used for training. He'd always encouraged Alex's socialization time with the other dogs and smiled as his partner headed toward two other members of K-9 teams. Loud barks and leaps onto each other's backs indicated both greetings and the time to play, and Donovan couldn't help but smile at the happy tail wags of his partner.

It was a huge contrast to his own confusion.

Confusion that sat squarely in the knowing eyes of Bellamy Reeves.

She'd already headed for one of the trainers and a group of puppies scampering around the yard. Her diverted attention gave him the reprieve he needed to analyze his thoughts.

What had happened on the drive down?

He and Alex had been with her for four days. Four agonizing days in which he'd diligently ignored the interest that simmered between them in favor of focusing on the task at hand.

Keeping her safe.

Clearly the sexual tension must have gotten to him because here he was, less than a week in her company, and he was like a singing canary.

He never spoke of his family or his feelings of inadequacy as an adopted member of the Colton clan. Yet there he went, spilling his guts to Bellamy like he'd known her for years.

The Coltons took you just the way you were. You're the one who doesn't want to accept that.

Her words continued to roll through and roil up his thoughts. Was it merely a matter of acceptance? Or was that too convenient an explanation?

No matter how much love his parents had lavished on him, they couldn't change the fact that his biological parents had left him. The people who were supposed to love him most had abandoned him in some rich family's barn, hoping and depending on the kindness of strangers. Wealthy ones, who could easily take on another mouth and who would be unlikely to abandon him a second time.

That wasn't a slight on Hays and Josephine, but a fact of his existence.

So why did it so often feel like punishment to the people who'd promised to love him the most?

Here he was, encouraging Bellamy to take the comfort and help of her sister, yet he'd been unable to do the same. Biological or not, his parents had shown their love in myriad ways since his infancy. The day they'd taken him in and given him a home was only the first.

So how did he begin to change? The helplessness he sensed in Bellamy—that question of where to start

with her sister—was the same for him. He'd been distant for so long he had no idea where to close the gaps.

No idea of even where to try.

With one last look at Alex, Donovan headed back
into the main building. His desk at the K-9 center had
all the same equipment and latest software as police
headquarters and he was determined to do some digging on Lone Star Pharmaceutical. The company had
an outstanding reputation, but the contents of Bellamy's
email continued to nag at him. It was a clue that couldn't
be dismissed or ignored.

If the corporation was involved in some bad dealing, he owed it to the investigation to tug that line and
tug it hard. Deliberately mismanaging the vital supply of vaccines was a crime and a health hazard and
no one, no matter how powerful, should be allowed to
get away with that.

Since Bellamy was still in the courtyard, safe with
the trainers, he wanted to take a few minutes to tug
those lines.

In moments he had several articles pulled up on
Lone Star Pharmaceutical and its founder, Sutton Taylor. The man was well-known in and around Whisperwood, and Donovan was humbled to realize he only
recognized the man peripherally. That knowledge only
reinforced his earlier thoughts of his family, another
proof point that he was out of the loop with his hometown news, gossip and local politics.

Donovan scanned article after article, getting a
sense of the man, before shifting to some of the more
telling websites. Anonymous reviews on those job sites
where people said what they really thought of their employer, Austin area gossip sites and even a few posts on

Everything's Blogger in Texas, a blog that had shown zealous attention to his extended family in the past.

The additional sites provided layers and context to his profile of Sutton Taylor, including a subtle thread of the man as something of a lothario.

He supposed it went with the territory—a powerful man with a powerful job—but it smacked of cliché at the same time. He wasn't a man who'd ever understood the appeal of cheating. You either wanted to be with the person you were with or not. It seemed awfully low to string them along when it was easier just to get out of the relationship and start a fresh one.

Was it pragmatic?

Or maybe it was a sign he thought relationships were too disposable?

Either way, Donovan knew it was how he was wired. He'd had several relationships over the years that had simply run their course. Nowhere during that time did he feel he needed to look elsewhere, but when it was time to leave it was time to leave.

Unbidden, an image of Bellamy the first time he met her filled his mind's eye. Bright-eyed and welcoming, she'd helped him with Alex and had been content to stand there in the general store parking lot as his small puppy had gotten sick. The moments that had followed had been even more special, talking and laughing and getting to know each other. He'd never forgotten that evening, nor the number of times he'd thought of her since.

Maybe it was those moments together that helped him see the person beneath the current pain. Or maybe it was just an attraction that hadn't been dulled by the ensuing years. Either way, he was attracted to her. It was inconvenient and not ideal, seeing as how he was working her case, but he *was* interested.

And he'd like to see where things might go between them.

A flash of awareness skittered through his mind as the night he met Bellamy came fully into focus. He'd been called away at the end to go to a nearby accident scene. Shifting gears on the computer, he minimized the articles on Sutton Taylor and pulled up his case files, logging backward until he found that night five years ago. In moments he had it up, the particulars of the accident coming back to him as he recalled the scene.

A drunk driver racing and swerving home from a holiday party. An older couple returning from an evening out. A small patch of road just off the main highway that lead into Whisperwood.

His gaze scanned the screen but Donovan already knew what he'd find.

Airlifted to Austin Memorial due to severe injuries: Daniel-Justice Reeves. Moved by ambulance to Austin Memorial for minor cuts and scrapes and further evaluation: Virginia Reeves.

He'd left Bellamy that night to go to the scene of her parents' accident. That was why he'd never seen her again.

It was the night her life shattered.

BELLAMY HELD THE now-sleeping puppy in her arms, loathe to let the little guy go. He was a smaller version of Alex, the K-9 facility trainer confirming for her that they had a lot of success with Labradors in the program. They'd rescued this one from a small flop in Austin and decided to raise him as their own. The trainer had already assured her they'd find a home for him if he ended up not being focused enough for the K-9 program and, on impulse, Bellamy had given the woman her phone number.

Her thoughts earlier in the week about having a dog had clearly taken root. She smiled ruefully as she headed into the building to find Donovan, but took joy in the idea that the pup had a future, no matter what happened to his time in K-9 training. They'd already named him Charlie and she thought it fit him to a T. That warm little body cuddled closer into her chest as she rounded the corner toward a large open-office area, and she bent down to smell his sweet little puppy head.

Oh yes, this was the right idea. And if Charlie ended up being a fit for K-9, Bellamy had been promised visiting privileges and the name of a rescue organization in Austin that would love to have another ready adopter on their list.

She entered the staff room and saw Donovan hunched over a desk. Winter sunlight streamed into the room, backlighting his broad frame as he focused on his screen. It made for an odd tableau and something in the set of his shoulders pulled her up short.

"Donovan? Is everything okay?" The puppy stirred lightly at her voice but quickly snuggled back into her arms.

He turned from the screen, his dark eyes shuttered. His expression was enough to have her moving forward. Something *was* wrong.

"What is it?"

"I'm sorry."

"For what? Did something happen?"

The puppy did stir then, either sensing her confusion or from a subtle tightening in her arms. He wriggled as his head lifted and she pulled him close, attempting to soothe him.

Since Donovan's attention had been on his computer, she veered there, surprised when he backed up to give her access to the screen.

"Bellamy, I'm sorry."

She scanned the screen and recognized the words, but didn't understand why Donovan had the record of her parents' accident pulled up. "Why do you have this?"

"It's my case file. That night. The night I met you when Alex got sick. We were talking and then I had to leave abruptly to go to an accident scene."

His words rattled around her brain like a loose pinball racking up points against the bumpers. "You? You were there?"

"I never realized it was your parents."

Her gaze roamed over the words once more, disbelief battling with the facts on the screen.

Drunk driver. Daniel-Justice Reeves. Virginia Reeves. Austin Memorial.

And the date all their lives changed.

Had he never put it together? Donovan had been called out to an accident, which was why he'd needed to rush off. There hadn't been one as massive as her parents' in years.

For the past week she'd simply assumed he knew and didn't want to hurt her by bringing it up.

But he'd had no idea.

She dropped into a nearby seat, the puppy now fully awake and squirming in her arms. He licked her face in obvious concern and she hugged him close, taking the comfort he offered.

"Are you okay?"

"I thought you knew. I took comfort that you were there."

"You did?"

"Of course. You saw them that night."

"Yes."

She'd always had a picture in her mind of what the accident must have been like, but didn't know the reality. She couldn't know what it smelled like or what it sounded like to hit another car with such force. She couldn't even begin to imagine.

For all his injuries, her father had seemingly moved past that point—past those horrid memories—but her mother never did. She'd struggled to sleep ever since the accident, to the point that Bellamy had considered a week with only one nightmare a good week.

And Donovan had been there.

"Did you help them?"

"We did all we could to keep your parents comfortable and steady until ambulance arrived."

"You were there for them."

Donovan only nodded, his lack of words somehow fitting.

What was he supposed to say?

It had been the same with everyone else in her life. People cared—they wanted to help and they definitely wanted to express sympathy—but in the end, there wasn't anything for them to do. Grief left a person helpless, but she'd learned it was no easier to comfort a grieving person. That had been the oddest part of her journey with her parents and had left the largest craters in her heart.

It had also served as the fuel to push others away.

She'd lost contact with her friends. She kept her colleagues at a distance, always claiming an excuse when she couldn't attend a happy hour or an event outside of work. Even her relationship with Maggie had suffered.

Years lost, along with some of the most important relationships in her life.

She hugged Charlie close, her attention shifting to Donovan. She'd been attracted to him five years before and a few days in his presence hadn't changed that. If anything, the concentrated time they'd spent together over the past week had only reinforced that initial attraction.

Was it coincidence that he'd come back into her life at a point where she needed a friend?

More to the point, did she want a friend, or did she want something more?

"Are you okay?" Donovan reached across and ran a finger over the top of Charlie's head. The little guy preened under the additional attention before lifting a paw to swat at Donovan's hand.

"I am. I've had a long time to get used to what happened. On some level, it's comforting to know you were there with them when they needed you. I've seen how capable you are. And I know how good it felt to have you there at LSP when we were dealing with my car." She reached out and laid a hand over his. "I'm glad you were there. Thank you."

"You're welcome."

Their gazes met and locked and Bellamy wondered,

with all that had happened in her life, how the world just fell away. The rest of it—her job, her car, even the threat at the house—it all seemed so far away.

In its place was something real and *present*.

She'd put off having a life for so long, it was star-tling to realize just how good it felt to be the object of someone's attention. To be the object of Donovan's attention.

"So you're okay?"

"I'm okay," she murmured, already anticipating the feel of his lips pressed to hers as he leaned in closer.

"Who's your friend?" His eyes dipped between them, the perusal intimate.

"You mean Charlie?" Her gaze dropped to the puppy, his excitement at having two humans so close causing him to wriggle even more.

Donovan kept a soothing hand on the dog's head, the steady attention holding him still, the back of his hand tantalizingly close to her breasts. "That's a good name. A good partner's name."

"He's the newest recruit for the K-9 program."

"Can you can give him his first lesson?"

"His lesson?"

Donovan moved even closer, his lips drawing nearer. "You think you can hold him still while I kiss you?"

A shot of heat traveled the length of her spine before spreading through her entire body. "I'll do my best."

The last coherent thought she had was that Dono-van Colton was doing *his* best.

The press of lips against hers was both firm and yielding, the perfect mix of give-and-take. He kept a calming hand on the puppy, his other hand settling against her hip. His fingers teased the top of her slacks where her waistband met flesh, a tantalizing brush against her skin.

But his mouth. Oh, the wondrous responses he could create with the greatest of ease.

Bellamy fed on his attentions, the sweet push-pull of desire fueled by their sensual play of tongues and the light moans each drew from the other. His fingers continued to trace light patterns against her skin, featherlight yet deeply powerful as her body heated at the simple touch.

She briefly questioned if her response was tied to how long it had been since her last relationship, but even she wasn't silly enough to think any man could compare to Donovan. Strong. Sure. Safe.

Capable.

Those attributes and so many more.

Charlie had stayed still, somehow sensing the humans needed a moment, but the waiting finally got to him. The combination of active puppy and a body that was going limp from Donovan's sexy ministrations got the better of her and Bellamy stepped back from the kiss before she lost her hold on Charlie.

"Whoa there. Hang on." Donovan took him easily, transferring the bundle of energy into his arms and holding the dog as if he weighed nothing. He lifted him up and stared him in the eye but kept his voice gentle. "Way to ruin the mood, little man."

Charlie only wagged his tail even harder, his tongue lapping into the air as his little body wiggled from his excitement.

"He looks very remorseful." Bellamy giggled, the small, wiggly body too cute to resist.

"I think we may also be getting the universal signal

to go outside. I'll be right back. There's something I want to show you anyway."

Bellamy watched Donovan go, struck once again by his gentle nature with animals. Even at the risk of wearing puppy pee or something even less desirable, he had a soothing way about him and kept Charlie close.

She stood there for a few moments, absorbing what had just happened. The intensity of the kiss. And the pure joy of being in Donovan's arms. Even the solicitous way he'd worried over her parents.

The computer screen still had all the information on her parents' accident and Bellamy scanned it again, doing her level best to read it with detachment. She knew the case well, but read through Donovan's impressions of the night and what he'd contributed to the report. His description of the scene matched the final crime report. So did the on-scene reconstruction.

"You sure you're okay with that?"

"I'm good." Bellamy glanced back over her shoulder, pleased to see Donovan was still dry. "No accidents before you got him outside?"

"It was close but Charlie showed admirable control. He also ran off to play with the big guys after doing his business so I'll leave it to Alex to keep an eye on him for a while."

"Alex is good with other dogs."

"He is. The socializing is good for him and so's the time outside. We're lucky to have pretty decent winter months here in Austin but I never take them fully for granted. Every opportunity to get him out here is time well spent for him."

The time at the K-9 facility obviously did Donovan good, too. He was more relaxed here. More at ease.

Was that because this was his professional home or was it because he wasn't comfortable in Whisperwood? His earlier comments about his family still lingered, but Bellamy chickened out before she could ask him about them.

There was a sweet vibe between them for the moment, a by-product of the kiss and the puppy, and she was loath to mar that in any way.

"Was there something you wanted to show me?"

"What do you know about Sutton Taylor?"

"The CEO of LSP?"

Donovan dragged over a chair from a nearby desk and pulled it up next to her and took a seat. "The same."

"I know him peripherally. Once a year all the departments present to him. Given how long I've been at LSP, he knows my name. I've had a few encounters with him at annual meetings and at the company picnic and I had to take him through a financial file once all on my own."

"What were your impressions of him?"

"He's incredibly well respected. He built LSP from the ground up, using some seed money he'd made early on in pharmaceutical sales. He's grown the business from there."

"That's good." Donovan nodded. "But what are your impressions of him, who he is as a person?"

"Oh. Well, I'm not sure I ever thought about it." She stopped as one of those rare meetings came back to her. "That's not entirely true. I remember this one time. We were waiting for a meeting to start and several of us were in line to get coffee and breakfast."

Donovan's attention never wavered at what she felt was a silly story. "Go on."

"So we're in line and because I had fiddled with a few pages of my presentation I was at the back of it. And I could see how Sutton admired one of my colleagues. I know men look at women. Heck, women look at men. It's natural. But most people aren't so—" She did break off then. "Most people aren't so obvious about it. And all I could think was that this was the founder of the company and he was ogling this woman like he was a fifteen-year-old boy."

"Do you think others noticed?"

"If they did, no one said anything. But there was just this quality about it all that I found disappointing. Like he should be above that somehow."

"Do you think he's behind the supply management and price-fixing?"

Bellamy wanted to dismiss it but gave the question her attention. "Why would he do that?"

"One of the two greatest motivators in the world. Money."

"What's the other?" The question was out before she could check it and his answer came winging back on a wry grin.

"Sex."

"Of course."

"Which brings me to my other question about Mr. Sutton Taylor. Take a look at these." Donovan clicked through several browser windows he'd opened, pointing out various elements that had caught his attention on each page with the mouse. "See here and here and here. All suggest, either in a veiled manner or in the case of that blog right out in the open, what a ladies' man he is. All reinforce the story you just shared."

Bellamy considered the assessment, weighing her answer. "I guess others have seen what I have."

"You're not ruining his reputation to answer honestly. Especially not if it will help us get to the bottom of what's going on."

It still felt like a betrayal of some sort, but Bellamy knew he was right. More, she was in the middle of this now whether she liked it or not and she had a right to take care of herself.

"He's very highly regarded for all he's built LSP into, but if I'm being honest, people do talk about his wilder side. Apparently he's had a wandering eye for decades now. His wife passed a little over a year ago, but rumor has been that she always turned a blind eye."

"Behavior like that might be enough to piss someone off."

"And give them access to our drug supply chain?" She shook her head, the notion simply not possible. "No way. There are too many people involved. Too many steps in the process. The sheer amount of government reporting we do on the various drugs we produce makes that virtually impossible."

"So we're back to the email as a way to ruin corporate reputation, not as fact."

She held up a hand. "Wait a minute. There's an easy way to find out if this is reputation or reality. Hang on."

Fifteen minutes later, Bellamy hung up the phone and tapped the notepad she'd scribbled onto. After five calls to pharmacy chains she knew LSP provided flu vaccine for, all confirmed they were out of it.

"Five for five?"

"Yep." She tapped the pad. "No one has the vaccine.

Once they got past their initial supplies in September and October, all were asked to pay highway robbery to reorder. And I know there's plenty of vaccine. Our supply is manufactured to ensure it."

"And no one at work has mentioned this?"

Bellamy considered Donovan's question, reviewing it through the new lens uncovered by the calls. "The office has been on a lighter schedule because of the holiday and I didn't give it much thought, but one of my colleagues was complaining in the lunch line a few weeks ago. He mentioned how he'd fielded several calls from field reps complaining about problems with orders. Only when he went back to look at the manifests, everything appeared to have delivered in full."

"So where's the gap?"

"Exactly."

Her gaze drifted back to the computer screen and a small link at the bottom of the article currently facing them from Donovan's screen. "What does that say?" She pointed to the link before reaching for the mouse to click on it.

A new window popped open out of the existing one, a small blurb on the blog they were already looking at.

Sutton Taylor in hospital with mysterious illness. Family worried the Hill Country's most powerful CEO is at death's door.

"Death's door? What?" Bellamy scanned the article quickly, trying to decipher through the gossip and the innuendo to see what she could discover. "It says here he's been ill for some time until being checked into a private facility between Whisperwood and Austin earlier this month."

"This site is known for stretching the truth. Has he been seen at work? Or has anything been mentioned about an illness?"

"Not at all. Last I heard his son was boasting that his father was headed out on a well-deserved Mediterranean vacation for the holidays."

"Could be a cover-up."

"But why hide that from the employees?"

"Maybe they don't want anyone to panic or get upset? Or feel they can get away with anything if the boss is ill."

Bellamy stilled at Donovan's theories. While all were sound, they seemed so foreign.

So at odds with the company she'd known and loved for the past thirteen years.

"Did you remember something?"

"No, it's just that this doesn't seem possible. I've worked there for so many years. Maybe my loyalty to them has blinded me to their possible faults, but what we're talking about...corporate price-fixing? Putting millions of lives at risk? How could I possibly have worked for a company who saw that as a way to turn a profit?"

"I'm sorry, Bellamy. Really, I am. You've lost a lot and this is only adding to that burden."

While she appreciated the sympathy more than she could say, it was way more than a burden. Had she truly spent nearly all of her adult life working for a company that was so profit driven they'd violated the core tenets of their business—to make people well?

"It's a lot to digest, that's all."

"Then why don't we do something to take your mind off of it? Staring at these articles isn't going to bring any answers. Maybe something fun and different would be a better idea."

"Like what?"

"There's a neighborhood down off Lake Travis full of big beautiful homes that's known for their Christmas decorations. They're also known for their friendly neighborhood competition of putting holiday inflatables on the front lawn."

"Sounds classy."

"Apparently it started as a prank from one house to another and morphed into a neighborhood joke. Now that they get over twenty thousand visitors a season, everyone decided to get in the act. Especially when they started charging admission for a local charity."

She hadn't been full of a single drop of holiday cheer this season, but something about the promise of goofy inflatable lawn decorations and bright, shiny lights felt like the right idea.

"Can Alex come along?"

"As if I'd leave him behind. Though I have to warn you, he's a bit of a spoilsport."

"Oh?"

"With all the running around he's done today, he's going to be asleep before we leave the K-9 training center."

"Poor baby. He'll miss all the fun."

Donovan leaned forward, a grin on his face as he whispered in a conspiratorial tone. "Shh. It's probably for the best. There's one house with a decoration of a dog dressed like one of Santa's reindeer that will give him nightmares for a month."

"Then it's good I'm along. I can make sure his eyes are covered from the horror of lawn decorations gone awry."

Chapter Nine

It *was* good she was along. Even better, Donovan thought, it was nice to see a broad smile on Bellamy's face as they drove slowly past the brightly decorated houses and the laughable lawn decorations.

"That is not a pig in angel's wings."

"It most certainly is."

Bellamy's laughter filled the car, a soothing balm to what they'd shared earlier. Even with the difficult discussion of her parents at the K-9 center, she'd kept her equilibrium, but he hadn't heard her laugh. The sound was enticing. Sweet.

And thoroughly enchanting.

Is that what the kids were calling it nowadays, Colton?

Bellamy Reeves might be enchanting, but she was also sexy as hell, a fighter and a woman who had come to occupy far too many of his thoughts in far too short a time.

Had she ever fully left?

That notion had dogged him on and off, taking root fully when he reviewed the case file on her parents. He *had* thought about her over the years. He'd be a liar if he said it was a strong, desperate sort of yearning, but he hadn't forgotten her.

He'd also remembered the easy conversation and sexy chemistry from the night they'd met with a certain sort of fondness. It was a sweet memory and he'd enjoyed pulling it out every so often, polishing it off and reflecting in the glow.

But seeing her again was something else entirely.

She was a beautiful woman and despite the understanding that her life was in tremendous turmoil, he couldn't keep denying his interest.

"There's a Santa decorating a tree in his boxer shorts. And over there is another pig but this one is in reindeer antlers. What is with this neighborhood?"

"I think it's a combination of fierce competition and a lot of money to burn. A lot of these lawn decorations are custom-made. This is one of the wealthiest neighborhoods in Austin."

"It sure is fun." She hesitated for a moment, and he might not have realized it if he weren't stopped behind a line of cars that had already slowed in front of them. "And I don't know. It's frivolous but they're obviously excited to share it with others. I think if you have money it's not so bad if you're willing to share it."

"Not everyone feels that way."

"No, I suppose they don't," she mused. "I'm certainly not wealthy. My parents got by at best and the only reason I have my house is because my parents' insurance settlement paid for it for me. But it seems that if you are fortunate enough to end up provided for, it's only right to share what you have. I love that all this fun also contributes to charity."

They drove on in quiet contemplation, occasionally

pointing out a certain house or a specific decoration, but otherwise not speaking. Donovan appreciated that they could spend time together silently, but also wondered what she was thinking.

He waited until they'd cleared the traffic and pulled out onto the road that would lead them back to Whisperwood before speaking again. "I know it's not much, but maybe it is a little burst of Christmas cheer."

"Thanks for that. It was nice to forget for a little while."

"Is that all?" A small shot burrowed beneath his breastbone. He'd hoped to do more than just allow her to forget for a while. Donovan had been intent on helping her make a new memory—something to hold close to her heart—even if the rest of her life still had more holes than she'd ever imagined.

"You know, your life's not over."

"Excuse me?"

"Your life. Your opportunity at happiness. It's not over because your parents died."

The warm moments they'd experienced on the drive through the pretty neighborhood vanished, melting away like ice on a summer Texas afternoon. In its place was a layer of cool that would give that same ice a run for its money.

"Are you actually lecturing me on grief?"

"I'm suggesting you have a right to live. Is that wrong?"

"Not at all. In fact, I think it makes perfect sense coming from you."

Donovan heard the warning signs. They all but leaped out at him, yet he pressed on. "Why's that?"

"Do you honestly think I'd take advice on grief and

the loss of my parents, at the holidays no less, from a man who can't be bothered to spend time with his own?"

"My family is my business."

"Yes, they are your business. They're also alive and well and interested in sharing your life, yet you hold them at arm's length."

Again, Donovan saw the red flag waving boldly in front of him and he barreled right on through, heedless of the consequences. "Like your relationship with your sister?"

"Maggie abandoned us."

"I was abandoned!"

The words slipped out, harsh and violent in the closed cabin of his SUV. Up to that moment, Alex had lay sleeping in the back seat, but he sat up at the rising tenor of their words. But it was the harsh emotion that ripped from somewhere around Donovan's stomach that had Alex nosing forward, poking at his triceps where Donovan had his arm resting on the console.

"Shh, buddy. Go back to sleep."

Alex was undeterred and sat straight and tall in the back seat, unwilling to lay down.

Neither he nor Bellamy said a word as he drove steadily on toward Whisperwood, and it was only when they neared the city limits that she finally spoke. "I'm not suggesting your feelings aren't legitimate. You've lived with the knowledge of being left by your biological parents. But what I don't understand is why you punish the family who loves you. They're a gift. And there will come a day when you can't take any of it back. When they won't be here any longer."

"They took me in out of duty."

"Isn't duty a form of love?"

The framing of that caught him up short. Duty as love? "It sounds like a chore."

"Caring for Alex is a duty. Yet you love him and you do it willingly. My parents were infirm and it was my duty to help them. Yet I did it with love. Helping others, taking them in, seeing them through the things that are hard—they're the *duties* we take on for the people we love."

Her words humbled him. All the way down deep, in the places he'd kept buried for so long Donovan had convinced himself they'd finally vanished, was a rising sense of remorse.

Had he been that selfish?

Yes, he had.

Worse, he'd thrown his family's love back in their faces, claiming that it was somehow less than or unworthy. He'd rejected them and they'd done nothing but love him. The knowledge was humbling. But more than that, it was enlightening.

The reality he'd spent his life running from was the one place where he truly belonged.

SUTTON TAYLOR SCROLLED through the news on his iPad and tried to make sense of what he was seeing on the screen. He'd felt like warmed-over bull crap for the past month—a sensation that had only grown worse by the day—but he was determined to rally.

Determined to get some of his damn strength back so he could figure out what was going on at his company. Jensen claimed to have everything under control, but if everything was under such tight reins, why did he have four emails on his personal account from long-time distributors asking where their flu vaccines were?

They'd shipped it months ago, the moment the vaccine came off the lines.

How were people out? Worse, he read the supply details himself. Signed the manifests for the eggs they needed to incubate the virus for the vaccines several months ago. They had *enough*, damn it.

So why was he sitting on multiple emails asking where the supply was? One even complained about pricing, which made no sense. They'd decided that back in March.

Head suddenly fuzzy, Sutton laid his tablet on the rolling tray that had become his constant companion and lay back into the pillows. He was so weak. He had moments of clarity but they were interspersed with long windows of fuzziness when he couldn't seem to grasp anything.

But he needed to grasp this.

Why were there no vaccines? Where had they gone?

Had he asked Jensen about it? The last time they talked—was it yesterday or today?—had he mentioned it to his boy? Or had he decided to keep it to himself?

The questions roiled in his mind, growing fainter like an echo that died out over the rolling Hill Country, but still he tried to hang on to the threads. Maybe he didn't ask the question. Maybe he wanted to see if Jensen asked him about suppliers calling looking for their vaccine.

Was that right?

The exhaustion that had dogged him for weeks finally gripped him in sharp claws and Sutton gave in.

He'd think about it tomorrow. He had to feel better tomorrow. It would all be clearer tomorrow.

It had to be.

BELLAMY STARED OUT the front window of Donovan's SUV and looked at her house, now lit up as man and dog traipsed through her small haven. Was it safe to go in?

And did she have any choice?

Every time they came home, the routine was the same.

Donovan and Alex had already gotten out to reconfirm the perimeter, then started in on the interior, leaving her with strict instructions to stay inside with locked doors and wait for them to come back. He'd also instructed her to keep her phone in her hand with his number already programmed in and her hand near the horn to quickly alert him to anyone outside.

It was a semicrude warning system, but she figured it would do the job if someone approached.

What she hadn't quite figured out was what had happened earlier. She'd pressed his buttons on their evening jaunt around Austin, that was for sure.

The real question, upon reflection, was why.

His relationship with his parents was none of her business. And even as she knew that—accepted it—she called BS on it, too. He'd started it all, poking around at her grief with an emotional stick. She'd simply defended herself in the age-old technique learned on the playground.

When mud's slung at your head, sling it right on back.

Which said very little about her if she was still employing playground tactics as a grown woman.

Donovan opened the front door and waved at her, hollering for her to stay in the car until he got there. She did as he asked and tried to juxtapose the protector marching toward her with the man who'd frustrated her less than an hour ago.

Your life. Your opportunity at happiness. It's not over because your parents died.

It was the holidays, for heaven's sake. The holidays were supposed to be hard for people who'd lost loved ones, and this was her first time through them without her mother or her father. A few bright lights and goofy lawn decorations couldn't change that.

Even if he'd tried really hard to give her something fun to focus on.

That thought caught her up short and whatever playground mud pie she was about to mentally sling died midtoss.

He'd *tried*.

And didn't that count for something? Something quite special, if she were being honest.

The door clicked open with his keyless remote and he opened her door. She swung her legs over, but stayed put in her seat.

"All clear. You got the Alex sniff of approval."

"Thank you."

"It's what we do."

She got out of the car but took his hand before he could move on. "For before. Thank you. You tried to show me a fun evening and I repaid you by saying some unkind things. I'm sorry for that."

"You don't have anything to apologize for."

"No, I think I do. The past months have been hard. Way harder than I expected, even, and I had more than enough time to prepare for this. But it was nice to escape for a while. To go see something fun and silly and happy."

The breeze that had swirled all day chose that moment to kick up, a sign that even with the warmer Texas days, it was still winter. She wrapped her arms around her waist at the sudden shot of cold. Donovan took her arms and pulled her close, the heat of his body an immediate balm against the wind. His head bent near hers, not quite touching, and she reveled in the loss of personal space.

A warm, manly scent filled her senses. A bit musky, a bit smoky, it made her think of warm fires on cold nights and she would have happily stood there in his arms for hours, if only for the opportunity to breathe him in.

"I think about the night we met," she murmured. "Not often, but I have thought about it."

"I have, too."

Ribbons of pleasure wrapped around her, delight at his words settling in her chest. "I can still see poor little Alex, sick on a few Legos."

"He did learn his lesson that night. He rarely picks up anything that's not food."

"That's good."

"And ensures far fewer messes in my house."

Once again, Bellamy marveled at how easy and freeing it was to be with Donovan. Their argument in the car had faded, and instead of creating a rift, it gave them another opportunity to connect. One of those small steps that paved the way toward a relationship.

Could something good come out of this confusing time? The small tingle that hovered beneath her skin reinforced just how much she hoped that might be possible.

A whisper of sound echoed from the direction of the darkened street and Donovan shifted, instantly alert. He pressed her back into the open car door before looking around, Alex leaping to attention. When man and dog remained still, neither moving, Bellamy whispered, "What is it?"

"I'm not sure. Let's get inside."

Her home was small, the driveway a modest distance from the front door. She often ran the length when she came home during a rainstorm and unless it was a soaker, rarely got too wet. But suddenly the stretch between the car and the front door seemed endless.

"I'll walk behind you and cover you to the front door."

"You can't—" She stilled at his unyielding gaze.

"Behind you. Let's go."

Bellamy respected his wishes, nerves racing the length of her spine and back again as she moved swiftly toward the front door. If something really was out there, wouldn't Alex have already started barking?

The thought had barely had time to land when a loud clatter cracked through the air, lighting up the night with noise. Donovan crushed her body to his before dropping them to the ground, absorbing the impact with his body.

Her breath whooshed out on a hard burst as Donovan quickly rolled over her, continuing to shield her with the length of his body. The heavy weight pressed her before it vanished. Then, before she could even register the rapid sensory changes, Donovan hollered instructions as he raced down the driveway, Alex at his heels. "Into the house, Bellamy! Now!"

She did as he asked, even as worry for him and Alex nearly blinded her as she fumbled her way through the front door. The precautions he'd taken to sweep the house upon their return had seemed silly at the time but now gave comfort. Her home was free of traps.

On the inside.

But an intruder lurked outside, and they seemed determined to find her, no matter where she was.

DONOVAN FOLLOWED ALEX, his partner's nose down and his focus solely on the hunt. Donovan kept up a steady stream of instructions to keep Alex focused on the scent, yet by his side. He didn't want to let him go and risk getting his partner shot.

The gunshots had been a surprise and they shouldn't have been. *Nothing* about this situation should be a surprise. Yet for reasons that defied description, the faceless threat to Bellamy continued to catch Donovan off guard.

She'd been targeted by a killer and it was time he not only accepted that fact, but took it for the serious threat it was. The crude construction of the bombs might suggest an amateur, but it also denoted determination, focus and a willingness to get the nefarious job done.

The escalation to gunshots only reinforced that determination.

He'd learned long ago that second-guessing himself in the middle of an op was the quickest way to lose focus, but the recriminations continued to pound in time with his steps. They'd been so focused on understanding why Bellamy was a target and what she might possibly know about the inner workings of LSP that they'd lost sight of the bigger concern.

Maybe she was simply the scapegoat.

The thought chilled him, but as the idea took shape and form in his mind, it grew clearer and more defined. By all accounts, the email that started this all shouldn't have even found its way to her. HR had paid no attention to her claims or even given her the benefit of due process. And perhaps the most telling, the initial attack against her happened on LSP property.

Everything centered on Lone Star Pharmaceutical and someone operating from behind its walls.

The online search earlier around Sutton Taylor played through his mind. Was the founder behind this? He'd built a successful company and could easily be maneuvering something like this from a distance. Money bought influence but it also bought professionals to do your dirty work.

Yet the job had smacked of an amateur from the start.

He paced behind Alex, moving off into the wooded area that surrounded her property line. He'd already reholstered his gun when they'd arrived back at Bellamy's home to do the property sweep and he kept a firm handle on it now. Even with that layer of protection, he was exposed. They'd barely cleared the woods when he called Alex to a halt.

He wanted to find his quarry but he was no good to Bellamy if he and Alex became sitting ducks for someone who saw them far more clearly than they could in return.

Alex stilled immediately, his training outweighing even the lure of the scent. With careful steps, Donovan backed them toward the road, his gaze roaming the area before him. Other than the briefest glimpse of their prey shortly after the gunshots, he had been totally blind to their assailant's whereabouts.

As his foot hit macadam, Donovan gave one final scan of the area. Then he turned and ran, zigzagging across the road to make himself harder to sight.

He didn't stop until he reached Bellamy's front door.

JENSEN LOWERED THE night vision goggles and watched the cop disappear into the night. The other hand that held the gun still trembled at his side, the realization the man had a dog an unexpected development. Those beasts knew scents and now the animal had his.

And that wasn't even his biggest problem. He knew the cop and remembered him from growing up in the same town.

Donovan Colton.

They hadn't been in school together, but everyone in town knew the Coltons. The Colton family regularly competed for their share of Whisperwood headlines, especially because of their black sheep cousins who lived a few towns over in Shadow Creek. Hays Colton had always downplayed that branch of the family, but family was family.

Wasn't that what this was all about, anyway?

He was the rightful heir to LSP. The company was his and nothing would stop him from securing his legacy.

Bellamy Reeves had been the perfect target. But as he watched Donovan Colton fade into the night, he knew the game had just taken on a new dimension. Cops didn't drive their caseloads around town in their cars. Nor did they hover over them in ways that suggested a far more intimate relationship than that of a protector.

But what were the odds?

The question both amused and frustrated as Jensen considered Donovan Colton. The man was a bright, shining example of why Jensen had started on this path to begin with.

It was time to go to ground, regroup and figure out how to manage this added dimension. He needed more information about Colton.

And then he'd take out the woman and the man who'd become her shadow.

Chapter Ten

Bellamy had hot coffee waiting and about a million questions.

"Are you okay? What happened? Was someone out there? I didn't hear any more gunshots."

Donovan had braced for the questions but hadn't prepared himself for the rush of need that poured through him at the sight of her.

"Donovan? Did you see anyone?"

With careful movements, he ensured his gun was safely holstered and removed the piece, setting it on the middle of her dining room table next to the mug of coffee. He scanned the room, pleased to see the curtains were already drawn on all the windows. Then he released Alex so his partner could get to the water and food that already occupied a place of prominence on Bellamy's kitchen floor.

Only when he'd done all that and realized his blood still pounded and his hands still shook with nervous energy did Donovan take what he needed. On a groan, he reached for her and dragged her close, burying his face in her neck and inhaling her. She was safe. Whole.

Untouched.

"Donovan." His name was a whisper where she

brushed her lips against his hair. "You're okay. I'm so glad you're okay."

He moved fast, the moment of comfort flashing over to a desperate, achy need that threatened to consume him as he took her mouth. She matched him, her lips meeting his in immediate surrender. He captured her hands, linking his fingers with hers, and gave the mutual need between them free rein.

There was power in the surrender, he realized as the kiss spun out. A power he'd never known or understood before. Dating. Relationships. All that had come before had been satisfying, yet functional.

But for Bellamy he burned.

Passion flared and Donovan kept his hold tight as he moved them both toward the couch. Dropping to the soft, well-worn cushions, he held her close as he draped her over his body so she straddled his lap. Their bodies pressed together intimately, a sign she was real and gloriously, physically present.

By unspoken agreement they never broke the connection of their lips, even as each explored the other. Her hands roamed over his chest, smoothing the lines of his T-shirt before dipping to pull the material from the waistband of his cargos. It gave easily, slipping over his body as her hands tugged the cotton higher and higher.

They broke the kiss only long enough for her to slip the shirt over his head, her mouth returning to his as her hands moved unerringly over his skin. Her explorations were tentative at first but grew bolder as the tips of her fingers circled the flat area of his nipples. Shots of heat moved from his chest to his groin, insistent darts of pleasure that both fulfilled even as they demanded more.

He wanted all of her.

But for the moment, he'd settle for touching her, feeling her skin beneath his fingers and pressing her to his chest.

His hands traveled the same path as hers, dragging the silk of her shirt from her slacks before shifting to work the line of buttons. One by one, those small pearls fell away to reveal soft skin. He grazed the swells of her breasts over the cups of her bra, the demands of his body building ever higher, ever tighter.

He wanted her. With everything he was, he wanted this woman who was so warm and responsive in his arms. Yet it was because he wanted her so much that he needed to hold back.

But heaven help him, he couldn't stay away from her.

Just a few minutes more. A bit more time to share what flared to life between them and reassure himself she was safe. A few more touches would hold him.

They'd have to.

His hands roamed over her breasts, the weight of her flesh heavy in his palms. He moved his thumbs over her nipples, the sensual play drawing a moan from deep in her throat.

The knowledge they needed to stop—that whatever flared to life when they were together couldn't be acted on further—nearly vanished like smoke at what pulsed and demanded between them. Donovan nearly gave in—nearly acquiesced to desire—when a loud bark echoed through Bellamy's living room.

Alex's war cry was fierce and immediate, effectively breaking the spell of desire that wound around him and Bellamy.

Need glazed her beautiful gray eyes, but rapidly gave way to the moment as she scrambled off his lap. Her motions were stiff but she moved quickly so he could get to Alex. His partner was already at the door, his bark deep and full as he stood guard.

"Alex." Donovan ordered him to quiet as he crossed to the dining room table and picked up his gun. He briefly thought to grab his shirt but refused to waste the time if their quarry lurked outside the house.

He'd already scoped out safe points in the house on his earlier sweep and knew the walls that framed the edge of the dining room were the most secure place. There were no windows in the room, and the short walls that set off the entrance archway would provide additional protection from the front door.

"Bellamy, please get behind the dining room wall. I'll let you know when it's safe to come out."

"Get behind—"

"Now, please."

The adrenaline that had carried him into the house fewer than twenty minutes before spiked once again, a heady cocktail that fired the blood. Alex had remained in place at the door, a ferocious protector who would go through the entrance first to protect his humans. The thought humbled Donovan as it always did, the animal's courage dwarfing that of many people he knew.

"Colton! It's Archer. Let me in."

The order was clear and at confirmation it was the chief, Bellamy scampered from behind the dining room wall toward her clothes.

"Bellamy—"

"I'm half-naked, Donovan, and the chief is here."
She hissed the words, color high on her cheeks, and
Donovan couldn't quite hide the grin. She did make an
awfully pretty picture, her skin flushed a sweet pink
while those gorgeous breasts pushed against the cups
of her bra that he hadn't managed to get off.

A quick glance down reminded him of his own decision to forgo his shirt and he pulled the door open to let
Archer in before striding back to get his clothes. Archer
was a quick study and likely would have known what
he and Bellamy had been doing, clothing be damned,
and there was no way Donovan was leaving his friend
to stand at the front door like a sitting duck.

Archer made a fuss over Alex, his gaze averted as
Donovan righted himself. If Bellamy's sudden appear-
ance from the corner of the dining room was at all a
surprise, Archer was too big a gentleman to show it.

"A neighbor down the way called in gunshots. You
wouldn't know anything about that, now, would you,
Colton?"

HEAT RACED FROM her neck to her face and back down
in increasing waves of embarrassment as Bellamy
smoothed her shirt over her hips. It was bad enough
she'd fallen into Donovan's arms like a woman starved,
but to be discovered by the chief of police added an
extra layer of mortification.

She and Donovan had been shot at and how did she
respond? By attacking him like some sex-starved fiend.

Although embarrassing, Chief Thompson's arrival
was perfect timing before she'd made an even bigger
mistake. She barely knew Donovan Colton. Yes, they'd

been thrown into a crazy situation. And yes, there was a base attraction.

But to act on it so quickly?

That was the recipe for a serious heartache once her attacker was caught and life went back to normal. She'd already accepted life had changed with the passing of her parents. Even her job could be overcome as she looked to find a new one.

But getting over Donovan Colton? Somehow she sensed that would be a near impossibility.

The man she'd met five years ago and had hoped to get to know better at the time had grown even more attractive and interesting. But their circumstances made it difficult to tell if there was truly something there or just the heat of close proximity in the midst of danger.

"Ms. Reeves? Are you okay?" Chief Thompson crossed to her, his concern evident. If he did have any thoughts about what she and Donovan had been doing—and she had no doubt he knew *exactly* what they'd been doing—it didn't show.

"I'm fine. Scared, but doing okay."

"Did you see who shot at you?"

"No. After we arrived home earlier, Donovan and Alex did a sweep of the house while I waited in the car. It was only after they came out with the all clear that we were shot at. Donovan took off after the shooter but he was gone."

The chief's attention shifted to Donovan. "Did you see him?"

"Nothing more than a fast-moving silhouette. I held Alex back as we didn't know what we were dealing with, although the suspect did have a man's build. Alex caught the scent and we'll follow it again in the morning and see what we turn up."

"I'll come back out to help you myself."

"We're leaving at first light."

"I do know how to wake up early, Colton."

Bellamy sensed the tension beneath byplay and knew there was something beyond the words. Donovan was embarrassed that he'd missed his quarry. On a base level, she understood that.

The chief, on the other hand, had increasingly impressed her. She'd believed him insensitive to her situation based on their first meeting, but now realized she'd misjudged his questions during the interview for something other than due diligence.

"I owe you an apology, Chief Thompson."

"Me? Why would you say that?"

"You seem upset about this situation."

"Of course I'm upset. There's a dangerous threat to my town and my people. I take that threat seriously and so does my entire department."

She nodded, her anger from that morning a distant memory. "After you questioned me. I thought you believed I was responsible. Now I see you were doing your job."

"You've come around pretty quickly."

"My father was a simple man, but he was quick to teach my sister and me that if you misread someone you owed it to them to fix the error."

Chief Thompson doffed his hat on a head nod. "Daniel-Justice was one of my favorite people in town. I was sorry when he was no longer able to manage the store and even sorrier when he passed. You have my promise I will do all I can to find who is doing this and to make sure you stay safe."

"I believe you will." Their subtle truce in place, Bellamy extended a hand. "I know it."

Feeling his firm handshake, Bellamy saw the promise in Chief Thompson's eyes matched the solemnity of his words. "Thank you, ma'am."

The chief left as fast as he'd arrived, promising to return at first light to go out with Donovan. He also assured her he'd bring along a deputy to stay with her while he and Donovan hunted for who was responsible. It was only after he'd left that Bellamy was left to face her earlier actions, the heat creeping up her neck once more.

She was alone with Donovan. Again. And while her clothing might be firmly resettled on her body, the memory of their flushed skin pressed intimately together was still fresh in her thoughts.

Too fresh, if the quivers that beat in tempo with her pulse were any indication. "You didn't need to do that. Before."

"Do what before?" Hesitation marked Donovan's tone even as his gaze shifted to the couch where they'd so recently explored each other.

"Racing off. Chasing the shooter. You could have been hurt. Or—" She broke off, the reality of what it meant for him to go off after a threat like he had. "Or worse. You could have been killed."

"I had Alex. We're a pretty good pair."

"Neither of you are a match for a crazy, determined person with a gun." She rubbed her hands over her arms, suddenly cold in a way she'd never experienced before. It pierced her skin and invaded her bones, a bleak sort of chill that made her wonder if she'd ever be warm again.

"That's why we only followed to the edge of the woods beyond your property. I know what I'm doing. And despite the threats so far, I will keep you safe. And myself in the process."

He moved closer as he spoke, each step punctuating his points, but Bellamy moved back in matched time, unwilling to give in to the nearly overpowering desire to return to his arms. She had to be strong—had to stand up and do this on her own. Donovan would catch whoever was doing this—of that she had no doubt. It was what would come after that time that worried her. Donovan would catch the perpetrator and then she'd be alone again.

The nearly desperate need for self-preservation had kicked in and she had to protect herself. When this was all over, Donovan would go back to his life and she to hers. It was time to start focusing on that.

"I, um. I should turn in."

"Of course." The small light in his gaze vanished, replaced with a subtle layer of confusion. "It's been a long day."

Bellamy grasped at the peace offering, clawing to keep her head above water and not come off like the most ungrateful bitch in the world. "Too long."

"I'm not tired yet, so I'll hang out here for a while, if that's all right?"

"Of course. Help yourself to the coffee or anything else you'd like."

"Sure. Thanks."

Then she made a run for it, the short trip to her bedroom seeming endless as she felt Donovan's gaze on her back. It was only when she closed her door and leaned back against it that Bellamy finally let the tears come.

In her entire life, she'd never needed anyone more than she needed Donovan Colton. But that way lay madness.

And a heartache she knew she'd never recover from.

Donovan settled down on the couch, Alex hopping up to curl at his side. The large blanket he kept for Alex was spread out beside him and his partner obediently stayed on it, his tail thumping lightly as he stared up at Donovan.

"Busy day, my friend."

The tail thumped a bit harder, whether it was agreement or the simple joy of sharing the day together. Donovan wasn't ever quite sure, but he appreciated the companionship all the same. He scratched Alex behind the ears, the dog's soulful brown eyes nearly rolling back into his head in ecstasy. He added a few additional belly rubs and a neck massage and in moments had a partner who snored like the dead perched beside him on the couch.

"And another one lost to Morpheus's powerful brew."

Donovan snagged his tablet from his bag and did a quick scan of his email, sending in a few updates on two of his cases in progress. His caseload was unusually light and he appreciated the extra time it gave him to watch over Bellamy, even as he struggled to find the right balance with her.

Had he scared her off? Or been too aggressive with the make-out session on the couch? Their stolen moments together had seemed mutual, but then she checked out after Archer had arrived, his tempting companion fading behind a very clear wall.

It served him right. He had no business taking advantage of her at such a vulnerable time and a bit of distance would be good for both of them. He'd allowed himself to think otherwise after spending several days in close proximity and the danger of the moment, but it was good Archer had arrived.

Wasn't it?

Well aware he didn't have the mental energy to figure it out, Donovan focused on the lingering questions that still dogged him about LSP instead. Whatever was going on, it had to be tied to Bellamy's job. The email. The car bomb placed at work. Even the way she was summarily fired without even a moment's consideration for her side of the story from Human Resources. All pointed toward something rotten at Lone Star Pharmaceutical.

Donovan pulled the same articles from earlier on Sutton Taylor, reading through the material, looking for any new insights. The man had helmed LSP for over thirty years. He held numerous patents in the field and was responsible for providing lifesaving drugs throughout the US and globally.

What would he gain from manipulating pricing on one of the most basic vaccines LSP produced?

Opening up a fresh search bar, Donovan tried a new angle. If there weren't overt answers with LSP, maybe there was something in the Sutton Taylor's personal life that would provide better insight. He tapped his way through a few searches before finally hitting pay dirt in an Austin lifestyle magazine article from about ten years before.

Donovan abstractly scratched Alex's head as he read the salient points out loud. "Married to high school sweetheart. One son, arriving later in their marriage. Provided extensive grants to the University of Texas medical school."

He kept scanning, the accolades for Taylor impressive. By all accounts the man was a veritable saint, his insistence on working for the public good a consistent mantra even as LSP accrued massive profits year over year.

Benevolence and profit. Was it really possible to maintain the two?

Donovan had a suspicious nature—he'd always believed it was what made him a good cop—and his senses were on high alert for what Taylor might be hiding. It was only as he clicked on yet another link that he remembered the blog from earlier. Toggling back to the *Everything's Blogger in Texas* post, he read through the list of gossip items that had followed Taylor throughout his professional life. Every article suggested the same thing, and all reinforced Bellamy's impressions, as well.

Sutton Taylor was a womanizer.

The blog was full of his conquests, with names, dates and, where those weren't available, a litany of insinuations. The lists also included three known illegitimate children, all claimed by Sutton Taylor as his own. Donovan read through the details, then clicked on the various links the blog provided. It was that last one that stopped him. An image of Taylor, dressed in a hunting outfit with a dog at his side.

The man's hand settled on the animal's head, his gun held against his hip with the other. The dog stared straight ahead, a faithful companion to his master. While the scene was different, it was such a clear match for his own photo for the K-9 team Donovan could only sit and stare.

Sutton's hair was longer where Donovan kept his short and cropped close to his head, but other than that the stance was the same. The jawline was the same. Even the shape of the man's hand where it cradled the dog's head was the same.

A subtle sense of awareness tightened his gut and Donovan flipped back through the other tabs he already had open, scrambling to find the blog and the list of dates. The tablet bumped against his knee as he swiped through various screens, jittery nerves jumping beneath his skin.

Was it actually possible? Could it be this obvious? Had the mystery of his birth been here in Whisperwood all along?

The blog provided confirmation and details on Taylor's three illegitimate children, all born over a ten-year period during his marriage and all provided for through legal means with a piece of his fortune. His son Jensen was the only child produced during his marriage.

Donovan vaguely remembered Jensen Taylor. The two of them didn't go to school together but Whisperwood was a small town and Taylor may have hung out with Donovan's older brother a time or two. Even with his limited memory, he did remember Jensen Taylor as one of the golden kids. Part of Whisperwood's elite, the younger Taylor had enjoyed the freedom his father's wealth provided and had run with a fast crowd. He and Donovan's brother hadn't stayed friends for long.

Was it possible the man was actually *his* brother?

It was a strange, disturbing punctuation mark to his weird thoughts about Sutton Taylor.

Had the man regretted one more illegitimate child and sought to deal with the problem by disposing of him in the Colton family barn? Even as he toyed with the idea, Donovan couldn't get any real enthusiasm behind it. Sutton Taylor was a powerful, wealthy man. He could do far better for his offspring—even the illegitimate ones—than dropping them off in a barn.

The wealthy had options, from farming unwanted children out to families or disposing of them through private adoption. Regardless of the path chosen, Taylor could have avoided ever having his name associated with an unwanted child—he didn't need to abandon a newborn infant to do it.

Nor did abandoning a baby follow pattern. The articles all reinforced the fact that Sutton Taylor had taken care of the children conceived outside his marriage.

Alex stirred next to him before lifting his head and placing it on Donovan's thigh. Warm brown eyes stared up at him, full of support and a devotion that never failed to humble him.

"Do you think it's possible?" Donovan whispered the question, testing it on his tongue and allowing it to expand and take shape in his mind's eye. Even with all the reasons against it, there was no accounting for human nature. Taylor was a wealthy married man with a reputation to protect. A family of his own he wouldn't want to expose to scorn or ridicule. Even if he hadn't cared for either of those things, thirty-plus years ago

Sutton Taylor was still building his empire. It might not have set well with investors if the young owner and businessman couldn't demonstrate even the slightest bit of control to keep his baser needs in his pants.

Hays and Josephine Colton were well-respected members of the community. They had a young, growing family of their own and were well-known residents of Whisperwood. They'd easily have the financial wherewithal to take on another child, and would be local so someone could keep an eye on the baby as it grew up.

Donovan considered the scenarios, testing them out to see what might stick. It wasn't a perfect theory, but it had some weight. Maybe what he needed was a good night's sleep and a fresh perspective after sleeping on it. When he woke up, perhaps he'd have answers. Like whether or not Sutton Taylor was his real father.

The one who'd abandoned him in a barn on Christmas morning, left to be raised by strangers.

Chapter Eleven

Donovan had no more answers at dawn than he'd had when he crawled into the small double bed in Bellamy's spare room six hours before. What he did have was a raging headache after a sleepless night and more questions than answers.

If Sutton Taylor was his father, who was his mother?

And if Sutton had abandoned him, had the woman spent the ensuing years looking for him?

Alternatively, what if Sutton didn't know at all? Maybe his mother had been the one to abandon him, leaving him to his fate in the Colton barn.

"You look like hell, Colton." Archer handed off a steaming to-go cup of coffee, his gaze irritatingly bright for 6:00 a.m.

"Thanks."

"You don't even look like warmed-over hell. You actually look like that special sort of tired reserved for first-year medical residents and parents of brand-new babies."

Donovan took a long sip of hot coffee and barely winced as the brew scalded his tongue, such was his need for the caffeine. "How would you know about either of those scenarios? Last time I checked you got queasy at the sight of blood and your ugly mug hasn't had a date in a year."

"Six months, but thanks for checking." Archer took a sip of his coffee and glanced toward the woods. He'd already left one of his deputies as backup in a cruiser parked in Bellamy's driveway before reiterating his intention that he wanted to go on the search himself. "I know Alex is good and all, but you think he can catch the scent again?"

"I know he can."

Donovan dropped to a crouch, his gaze level with Alex. "You ready to go to work?"

Alex's thick tail began its fast metronome thump against the ground and Donovan couldn't help but grin up at Archer. "Alex is ready. The real question is if you can keep up."

"Lead the way."

"Let's go get 'em, Alex."

The three of them took off in the direction of the copse of trees that surrounded Bellamy's property. The area was thickly wooded, though not nearly as overgrown as it had looked in the dark. Alex navigated it with surety, trailing over leaves, twigs and the occasional downed log as he pushed them onward, farther into the trees.

Donovan took it in, the air growing quiet as the foliage grew thicker. While a big part of him would have preferred to end this all the night before, he was still sure of the decision to return to Bellamy. Barreling into the trees, heedless of a man with a gun who potentially had a better view on them than they had in return, was a suicide mission.

"You come up with a motive yet?" Archer asked.

Donovan kept tight hold on Alex's leash, his focus on the dog's small signals that confirmed a change in direction or an increase in the intensity of the scent he tracked. His partner saw the world against the dimension of smell and Donovan had learned long ago to let him work against the pictures that world made.

"Money or power's my pick."

"Money's usually a good one. They teach you that at the academy?"

Donovan ran a tired hand over the back of his head. "First day, I think. Funny how it's a lesson that keeps repeating itself."

They tromped in silence for a few minutes, the only sounds Alex's thick sniffs and occasional whines from the back of his throat as he caught a fresh direction.

"I put in a warrant for access to LSP's tech," Archer spoke. "But I am hitting a wall so far. Between the holidays and a 'flimsy case' as Judge Carson told me, I'm not getting very far on diving into the LSP email server."

"Carson's tough."

"Yeah, but he's not wrong. I need something more than a printout of a suspicious email to go on."

"You been looking at anyone else? You and I both know Bellamy Reeves is innocent in all this." It was on the tip of Donovan's tongue to ask about Jensen Taylor but something held him back. His questions from the previous evening and his hunt for information on Sutton Taylor had left him exposed and raw, and Donovan wasn't quite ready to poke around that one.

Especially not with someone as astute as Archer Thompson.

"I've got notes to call Human Resources today.

Something about Bellamy's description of her time with the director kept ringing my bell. It feels funny, you know? Who gets fired on the spot for bringing something to HR's attention?"

"A guilty someone?" Donovan asked.

"Guilty on which side is my concern."

Archer's comment pulled Donovan up short and he tugged lightly on Alex's leash to pull him to a stop. "You think HR's got something?"

"I think it's awfully strange that Bellamy goes to HR to make a formal complaint and is not only fired but walks out to an explosive device in her car. I'm not much into coincidences, nor do I like situations where our victim appears to be bullied."

"So why'd you give her a hard time in your office?"

"To make sure she is a victim and not the puppet master behind the scenes."

Donovan chewed on that idea, the opportunity to bounce things off the chief a welcome distraction from his own thoughts. "I'm not a big conspiracy buff but the puppet master angle has legs."

"Don't you mean strings?"

Donovan only shook his head and wouldn't have been surprised to hear Alex groan at that one. "They clearly didn't make you chief on your rockin' sense of humor. But they did make you chief on your nose for bad guys. Who's in a position to pull those strings?"

"Offhand? I'd say bigwigs at LSP. Maybe a few enterprising drug distributors who have some of the biggest accounts in hand and already locked up. Maybe even a disgruntled employee who manages the supply chain high up."

"I've looked but haven't found anything to suggest LSP is in dire financial straits."

"Me, either." Archer crushed his coffee cup in his hand before shoving it into his back pocket. "Wall Street's happy with their quarterly and annual performances and their stock remains strong. Something like this puts that performance at risk instead of enhancing it."

"Not including the profit they might make in the meantime."

Archer shrugged. "Still seems awfully shortsighted. Why ruin the company reputation and long-term health for the sake of a few bucks in the short term? Especially if you're profitable to begin with."

"Back to our original motive?" Donovan asked. "Money."

"Short-term money versus long-term success, aka money. Still seems shortsighted to me."

Shortsighted, illegal and overconfident. Each description fit and suggested a person who had little self-control and more than their fair share of arrogance.

Which only brought Donovan right back to Sutton Taylor. The man had proven himself out of control and arrogant when it came to his personal choices, but in his business, he'd seemingly exercised control and long-term vision.

So why ruin that now?

SUTTON RAN HIS hands over the thin hospital blanket, his fingers tracing the weave over and over. He'd begun counting the interlocking squares, desperate to stay awake and focused. It was so hard to concentrate and he *needed* to concentrate.

Needed to stay alert.

More, he needed to figure out what was wrong.

He'd have windows of time when he understood something was the matter and then would fall back to sleep, groggy and unfocused, his body exhausted from the mere effort of thinking. But it had to stop.

Twelve. Thirteen. Fourteen.

He couldn't afford to sleep anymore. Like last night. What was he thinking about? And what had filled his dreams with oversize cars that floated in the air before exploding, their parts shattering like a firework?

Twenty. Twenty-one. Twenty-two.

Jensen. Wasn't he worried about his son? Sutton tried to focus on that as he kept counting, forcing himself to stay awake with the repetition.

Where was Jensen?

Forty-four. Forty-five. Forty-six.

Jensen was watching over LSP. But why was Jensen in charge? He hadn't shown a great aptitude for the business. In fact, some of his ideas were flat out wrong.

We need to focus on managing our production. Too much product floods the market, Dad. Scarcity is our friend.

We produce the drugs people need to get well. Why would I throttle production? We need to find opportunities to expand. To push past our production limits to get more into supply. To help more people.

Profit. Jensen had slapped him on the back with a barely concealed eye roll. *Profit is why.*

When had they discussed that? A few days ago? Or was it months?

Sutton stopped counting squares, his hands going still on the blanket. It *had* been months. Back in the spring when they were finalizing the formulary and the orders on the flu vaccine.

And now their suppliers didn't have enough vaccine?

Their suppliers. The emails. He'd read the emails last night.

Sutton reached for his phone where it lay on the rolling tray that sat beside the bed. He lifted the device, his hand shaking as he tried to turn it on. Damned phone, what was wrong? His hand shook as he stabbed at the small button at the base, only to see the phone screen black and lifeless.

Out of charge.

His hand shook harder as he tossed the phone back onto the tray. A loud beep started from the machine behind his head as his entire body began to shake. The dim lights in the room quavered, shimmering in and out of focus as several nurses came running through the door.

BELLAMY AVOIDED ONE more look out the front window, well aware of what she'd find. The deputy's car would still be in her driveway, the man perched behind the wheel with his gaze on the road. She was impressed by his diligence, even as she questioned how horribly bored he must be just sitting there.

For her.

Once again, that thought struck her. It had hit hard when she realized how focused Donovan was on keeping her safe and protected, but it extended to the broader Whisperwood police force. So many people trying to keep her safe from a killer.

Would they succeed?

Was it even possible to succeed against someone so determined?

Sick of pacing and worrying, she crossed her arms and tapped her fingers on her biceps. What else could she do? She'd already cleaned up the kitchen and freshened Alex's water and food for when he and Donovan returned. The beds were made and the living room had been straightened up. She'd even toyed with mopping the kitchen floor, which meant her boredom had reached unprecedented heights.

Still, her thoughts flipped and tumbled, one over the other and back again.

Who was behind all of this? And why had they targeted *her*?

When she stopped asking that question through the lens of the victimized—*Why me?*—she'd begun to ask different questions. It was less a question of why was this happening to her and, instead, why had she been targeted.

Did she know something? Or had she been inadvertently exposed to some sort of information that had made her an easy target?

Her laptop was closed and still sitting on the edge of the kitchen counter. She'd nearly glanced past it, her eyes roaming over the floor once more as she considered pulling out the mop when she refocused on the laptop.

Was it possible?

Reaching for it, she opened the lid and waited for the computer to come out of sleep mode. In moments, she had a browser window open and tapped in the familiar remote address that would put her into the cloud.

And access into her email.

Butterflies dive-bombed her stomach as she walked through each step. Technically she was no longer an employee. Which meant she had no right to log into the system and even less right to hunt through her email.

Which made it all the more imperative that she take what she could while she could.

Her latest password—HOLIDAYSSUCK, all one word—spilled easily from her fingers. She hit the return key, shocked and extraordinarily pleased when her email filled the screen.

She was in!

In HR's rush to fire her, they'd forgotten to go through the proper protocols to turn off her email and remote access. All standard when an employee was terminated.

Yet they'd forgotten to dismantle her accounts.

Well aware diving into her email didn't put her in a good light, Bellamy shrugged it off as the least of her problems. She sorted through the unread emails that had come in over the past few days. She passed notes about the holiday schedule, the latest financial reports for the prior week and even a note about using up benefits before the end of the year, scrolling toward the email that had started it all.

Staring at it with fresh eyes, she noticed there wasn't a named sender in the chronological listing of email. Instead, all she read was the word INTERNAL. Which was odd. She'd been at LSP long enough that she knew the form their email addresses took. There was no sender called INTERNAL.

Of course, no one sent anonymous email detailing corporate greed and illegal behavior, either.

Yet someone had sent this one.

She opened the email again, quickly sending a copy to her personal address before looking once more at the details she'd not paid enough attention to upon first viewing. She was no tech whiz, but she'd used enough software programs throughout her career that she figured the navigation bar at the top was the place to start.

The information command didn't provide any detail beyond the date and time sent. Ticking through the other options, she tried to open the actual sender's email address, only to find a string of gibberish that read like a garbled line of code.

Was there something in that? Something an expert could track back and use?

The peal of her cell phone pulled her from the screen and Bellamy practically dived for the device, desperately hoping it was Donovan telling her he was on his way back. Instead, her friend Rae's name flashed on the screen. They'd texted recently but hadn't spoken. Bellamy regretted her hasty info dump of what had happened the other day and wanted to minimize Rae's involvement in what was going on.

But ignoring her friend wasn't fair, either.

"Hey."

"You're lucky this week's one of the busiest at the store or I'd be camped out on your front lawn as we speak."

"Good morning to you, too."

"Your sister was in here last night. Told me that your car blew up."

"It didn't—"

Before she could protest, Rae pressed on. "Bell. The bomb squad was called and you've got protection detail at your house. What am I missing here?"

"I didn't want to worry you." *Or risk involving you in something that grows more dangerous by the hour.*

"I'm your friend. Of course I'm worried about you. And Maggie is beside herself."

"Maggie already read me the riot act."

"Good for her."

A small gasp caught in Bellamy's throat. "Don't tell me you're on her side."

"In this I am. I don't care what's in the past or how far apart you two have been. She's your sister and she's worried. Rightfully so."

Bellamy toyed with the track pad on her computer, the cursor circling the screen in time to the sweep of her finger. Rae had always been her rock, her supportive champion who was always on her side. To hear her defend Maggie was a major departure from her usual stalwart defense.

"Does the silence mean you're mad at me?"

"Of course not."

And she wasn't. But it did sting to hear her friend so easily defend her sister. She and Maggie had been on opposite sides for so long, it was startling to realize the sands beneath her feet might have shifted.

Did Maggie actually care about her?

She'd believed it once. The baby sister whom she loved and adored could do no wrong and Bellamy had believed their sibling bond would keep them close forever. Then her father had gotten ill and Maggie had grown more and more distant. It was easier to blame her or think poorly of her instead of trying to see her side of things.

And that was on her, Bellamy acknowledged. She had a right to her opinion and an even bigger right to disagree, but her unwillingness to hear Maggie's side sat squarely with her.

"So what's going on?" Rae's question pulled her back from her thoughts, and Bellamy pictured her friend up to her elbows in holiday inventory as she worked to get the general store open for the day.

"I wish I knew, Rae. Really, I wish I did. Things have gotten weird and scary."

"Is Donovan Colton with you?"

"You know about that?" Why did that bother her so much? Donovan wasn't her personal property and it wasn't exactly a secret he was helping her. Even with the pep talk and the silent acknowledgment not to get flustered about it, Bellamy couldn't quite hide her frustration. "Let me guess, Maggie told you."

"I didn't need Maggie to tell me. Marie in HR at LSP was in here yesterday. You were all she could talk about. You and the hot guy helping you."

Bellamy caught on the name, cycling through the people she knew at LSP. Marie was the woman who'd brought her files into Sally's office the day she went to HR.

"You know Marie? Do you know anything about her?"

"No more or less than I know about most people. She and her husband settled in Whisperwood about three years ago."

"And she told you what happened?"

"Quite happily. Told me some stuff had gone down at LSP and that HR took an employee to task. Unfairly, too." Rae's smile traveled through the phone. "I put two and two together that it was you. And when she started telling me about the hot cop seen around town with his dog, I took my two and two and multiplied them even further. Donovan Colton doesn't make it to Whisperwood all that often. The fact that he's stuck around is a testament to you."

"Why me?"

"There's no love lost between him and his family. Most of his trips through town are quick and functional at best. But from the gossip swirling around town, you've given him a new reason to stay."

"That's just silly. He was the one who got the dispatch call on my car and he's been helping me out. Nothing more."

"Are you sure?"

"Of course I'm sure."

"Then why do I hear that funny note in your voice?"

Bellamy flushed any sense of surprise or outrage from her tone, focused on keeping things as nonchalant as possible. "I don't have any funny notes."

"Yes, you do. You're sort of squeaky at the edges, like that time in freshman year you asked Bill Monroe to the Sadie Hawkins dance."

"I do not."

"I heard it again. You squeaked at the end of your protest. Which means you've got something juicy and interesting to share."

It was on the edge of her lips to protest before Bellamy pulled it back. Rae knew her well and would only take joy in continuing to push her buttons. So she switched gears and focused on why she hadn't called in the first place.

"Please promise me you'll be careful. Keep your ears open but don't ask any questions and don't give anyone the idea you and I have spoken."

The laughter that had characterized Rae's voice up to then vanished. "What's going on, Bellamy?"

"Promise me. Please. You need to be careful and you don't need to let on to anyone that we've communicated. Not until this is all taken care of."

"Taken care of? Who's taking care of it?"

"Please, Rae."

"Okay. I promise."

"Thanks. Now go do what you need to do and I'll call you in a few days."

"If you're sure?"

"Positive."

They said a few goodbyes and then hung up. As her phone switched off, Bellamy couldn't hide her concerns. The person who'd targeted her had made it clear they knew what she drove and where she lived. It would stand to reason they'd know who she was friends with, as well. And who her sister was.

Fear struck low in her gut, raw and icy cold. Not seeing eye to eye didn't mean she didn't love her sister. But could she get to Maggie in time? Reaching for her phone once more, she dialed Maggie's number and counted off the rings.

And wondered what it meant when her sister didn't pick up.

DONOVAN TOSSED HIS gear in the back of his SUV, frustrated with the wasted morning. They'd been out for over three hours and, other than going around in circles, Alex hadn't found anything useful. Or more to the point, their quarry had covered his tracks.

Even with a disappointing trek, Alex always got his treat when he was done. Donovan hunted for the container of bones he kept packed in the back of the car and pulled one out for his partner.

"I'm going in to work on the tech angle." Archer looked as frustrated as Donovan felt, and once again, he was struck by the man's commitment to the community of Whisperwood. "I still don't believe we haven't found a thing."

"Me, either." Archer waved his deputy on before crossing Bellamy's driveway to meet him.

"Wait." Donovan patted his gear, suddenly remembering the button he'd found in the sweep of Bellamy's car and tagged in an evidence bag. "I pulled this when I swept her car and tagged it."

"A button?"

"Off a man's shirt. A fancy one, I think."

Archer turned the bag over in his hands, tracing the thin disc. "I don't have the resources to hunt this down but it is another notch in Bellamy's favor. Where'd you find it?"

"Buried beneath the seat. I would have ignored it except for the fact that she was genuinely surprised to see it. Claimed that it didn't match anything she owned."

"You mentioned earlier this felt like an amateur job." The chief eyed the button once more. "Here's one more example that reinforces the point. No one even halfway decent at their job would risk losing something like this."

"It's clumsy. Lazy, too." Donovan nearly mentioned his suspicions about Sutton Taylor but held his tongue at the last minute. He had suspicions and nothing more. You didn't go around accusing men of Sutton Taylor's stature and standing in the community on a hunch.

Nor did you go around suggesting he was your missing father.

So Donovan waved Archer off instead, mulling over all he'd discovered. And while he considered all of it, he had a woman waiting for him.

One who might have the answers to his questions. And one who might help him figure out the mystery of his father. Donovan finished stowing his things when the sound of tires on pavement had him turning to see Maggie Corgan pulling up.

The woman was out of the car and around the hood, her perfect blond hair waving around her face in the morning breeze. "First it's a bomb and then it's gunshots? What is going on, Officer Colton? Who's after my sister?"

Donovan was struck once again by the sincerity in Maggie's eyes. The relationship between her and Bellamy might be strained, but he didn't think it was because Maggie didn't want one with her sister. "I'm working to find that out, ma'am."

"Why has she been targeted? None of this makes sense. She's the kindest, gentlest person. She's a hard worker and she's always loved working for LSP. I hate that she lives out here all by herself, but I know it's what she wanted. It's why—" Maggie broke off, her eyes widening.

"It's why what?"

"Nothing." Maggie waved an airy hand, the motion dismissive. "Nothing at all."

"Ms. Corgan." Donovan moved closer, curious to see a look of utter defeat in the woman's eyes. "Do you know something?"

Maggie shook her head, her gaze dropping to the sidewalk. "About what's happening to her? No."

"Then what are you talking about?"

"I tried the only way I knew how."

She broke off again, her slim form agitated as she twisted her hands and shifted from one high heel boot to another. "Tried what, Maggie?"

"I tried to marry the right person to have money for my father's treatments. It was the only way I knew how, and I thought James and I would be a good fit. He wanted a trophy wife and I never minded being a trophy all that much." She sighed, brushing her hair back. "I'm butchering this. Why don't I try again?"

Donovan waited as she gathered herself, suddenly curious to see the parallels between Bellamy and her sister. While he wanted to hear the entire story, he'd already sensed where Maggie was going. It was humbling to see what had changed that lone night he went off to an accident scene and all that had played out since. Two sisters, each driven to help their family.

Each stymied by pride.

There's a lesson in there, Colton.

The thought struck hard, an uncomfortable parallel to his own family relationships that he wasn't quite ready to explore.

"Things didn't work out the way I planned and James wasn't all that free with the checkbook. He gave me a bit as an allowance that I could funnel to my family after I bought the requisite clothing and shoes and my mother-in-law took pity and helped a bit once she knew what was going on. It wasn't enough, but it was something. And it gave me enough to get this house for Bellamy. Before it all—" Maggie hesitated again, her gaze roaming toward the house. "Bellamy thinks my parents left this to her, but they didn't. There wasn't any money from their estate left to leave her and I didn't want to take this from her. I know how important this house is to her. How important these memories are. So I worked with the lawyers to make it so."

"Why can't you tell her?"

"Because I can't. And you can't, either. Bellamy isn't interested in what I have to say and I'm not going to grovel for my sister's affection."

If Donovan thought the knowledge would put Bellamy at risk, there was nothing that would keep him silent, but he could hardly fault family relationships or go against them. "I won't."

"Thank you."

"But I do think you should tell her. There's love there. Between the two of you. It'd be a shame to miss an opportunity to build a relationship as adults."

Maggie's eyes narrowed, her mouth firming into a straight line. "I know your sister. She and I both worked on a Junior League project a few years back."

"Oh?"

"She mentioned her family on several occasions while we worked on that project. I know how important her family is to her and how much she'd like adult relationships with her siblings. I got the sense that she had that with all but one of them."

"I don't—"

"Things aren't always as simple." She laid a hand on his arm. "Even when they should be."

Bellamy chose that moment to come outside, her eyes shielded against the morning sun. Maggie waved at her, her smile bright. "Just catching up with Officer Colton. He's got things well in hand."

She moved back around to her car and climbed in, starting the car and pulling out before Bellamy had even crossed the yard.

"What was that about? Why did she leave?"

"I think she came to visit me. To make sure I'm handling your case well."

"Was she satisfied with what she found out?" Bellamy's gaze remained on the departing car as it sped down the street.

"I have no idea."

Donovan walked Bellamy back to the house, Maggie Corgan's parting words still heavy in his heart.

Things *weren't* always simple.

Even when they should be.

Chapter Twelve

Bellamy left several messages for Maggie over the next few days but hadn't managed to reach her sister. They exchanged a couple of texts every day and she tried to probe what Maggie's holiday plans were, even going so far as to invite her for Christmas dinner, but got a vague excuse about being busy.

Which stung.

She'd tried, hadn't she? Extended the olive branch and attempted to repair things and got a big fat slap in the face for her efforts.

It was one more layer of frustration overtop of the rest of her life. Donovan and Alex had been in her home for nearly a week and they were no closer to finding the person behind the attacks on her than they'd been since man and dog moved in.

Other than the pervasive sense of being watched, nothing else had happened to justify Donovan and Alex's ongoing presence in her home.

And the lack of information or movement on her case had everyone on edge.

She, Donovan and Alex made daily trips into Austin, spending time at the K-9 center and getting some distance from Whisperwood, but each night they'd return, no further on her case than when they'd started. It was maddening.

Even more frustrating was the fact that each night they went through this weird, awkward good-night that sent her to her room alone while Donovan and Alex headed for her spare room.

Maddening.

Bellamy snapped the lid of her laptop closed. She'd just paid off her last remaining December bill and was angry by the ever-dwindling number in her bank account. She couldn't be without a job forever, nor could she stand sitting around much longer.

But for the moment she was in a holding pattern.

Her LSP email still worked and she and Donovan had explored all they could find from a distance, but the system was fairly locked down in terms of using it as a mechanism into the inner workings of LSP.

Donovan had sent her email to one of their digital forensics experts to work through the signatures that sat behind the data but the woman had found precious little to go on, and without a warrant for LSP's data they didn't get very far. Which only added to the soup of frustration that was her life.

"It's Christmas Eve. Would you like to go look at lights again? I hear they've got a big holiday festival south of Austin as you head toward San Antonio." Donovan padded into the kitchen, his feet bare beneath jeans that hugged his backside and a black T-shirt that made her mouth water. The man had limited tastes and he'd already washed and recycled several T-shirts that hugged his chest, but the jeans were a mainstay.

Which also only added to her general sense of irritability.

The man was mouthwateringly attractive and he hadn't laid a hand on her since their interrupted make-out session on her couch. Where she'd first thought that was a good thing, as each day went by she'd grown less and less convinced.

"I know it's Christmas Eve. And attempting to cheer me up with shiny lights isn't the answer."

"Okay." Donovan shrugged and poured himself a fresh cup of coffee.

"And you can get rid of the attitude while you're at it. I know it's boring as a tomb around here. Why don't you go back to your family or just go home? It's silly for you to sit here day after day. No one's going to attack me for Christmas."

She'd rehearsed the speech in her head, desperate for her life to return to some sense of normalcy, but had to admit to herself that it didn't come out quite as she'd planned. In her mind, it was competent and confident, setting the tone for how they'd move forward. In reality, it had come out edgy and whiny, with a side of bitchy that didn't speak well of her, especially when she'd stood up and fumbled the chair behind her.

No, it didn't speak well of her at all.

"You want me to leave?" Donovan asked.

"Do you really want to stay?"

"I want you to be safe."

"Since the incidents stopped, it's hard to feel like I'm in danger."

"You didn't answer my question." He left his mug on the counter and moved closer, his hands firmly at his side even as he moved up into her space. "Do you want me to leave, Bellamy?"

"I don't—" The words stuck in her throat when his hand lifted to her stomach, the tip of his finger tracing the skin there. The touch was light but it carried the impact of an atom bomb, fanning the flames of attraction that she'd tried desperately to quell over the past week.

Whatever had happened on the couch was a moment in time. A crazy moment of abandon that didn't need to be repeated.

Hadn't she told herself that over and over this past week? More than that, hadn't she seen firsthand how hard Donovan worked and how committed he was to her and to his caseload? He stayed with her, uprooting his own life while still digging into her case. Even with all that, he remained focused on his other responsibilities, as well. Their daily drives to the K-9 center had shown his dedication to Alex and keeping him fit and well trained. Even the things he'd shared with her over coffee each evening had pulled them closer.

He'd opened up about his family a bit more, usually in the guise of probing her about Maggie, but it was sharing all the same. And a few nights before he'd blown her mind when he shared his theories about Sutton Taylor. His comments hadn't moved far from her thoughts, the image of the man she knew as leader of LSP as Donovan's biological father. She struggled to put the two together, yet as she listened to his points, had to admit his theory had merit.

The fact they couldn't find Sutton Taylor to speak to the man directly had only added to the questions around LSP's leader. The chief's inquiries to Lone Star Pharmaceutical had gone unanswered, Sally Borne's dismissal of requests growing increasingly uncooperative.

Where was the man? Holidays or not, CEOs never went so far away as to be unreachable. Yet the man seemed to be off the grid and every outreach made to local hospitals—even the exclusive ones—hadn't turned up any leads.

All the questions and conversation had brought them closer, yet until this very moment, Donovan hadn't so much as touched her. Nor had his dark gaze turned heated, not once. And neither had he attempted to kiss her again.

So what were they doing here?

Yes, she was under his protection, but she'd never heard of anyone getting a personalized police protector who moved in. He'd gone above and beyond and it was getting more and more difficult to understand why.

"What are you doing?"

A small smile tilted his lips as he continued pressing his finger slightly against her stomach. "Nothing."

"Are you bored?"

"You seem to be."

"Are you?"

"Whatever I am, Bellamy, I can assure you it isn't bored."

She lifted his gaze from the mesmerizing play of his finger. "Then what are you?"

"Truth?"

"Of course."

"I want you and I'm not sure I can do the right thing by you any longer."

"You're—"

The right thing? Had he been purposely keeping his distance?

He waited while she worked through the details, punctuating his point when she gazed up at him once again. "You're under my protection. You're my responsibility. It would hardly do to act on our attraction."

"Why not?"

"Because it's unprofessional. And a conflict. And—"

She moved into his body, wrapping her arms around his neck to pull him close. All the confusion and anger and frustration of the past week faded as he opened his arms and pulled her close. "And completely wonderful, Donovan Colton."

"It's nearly killed me this past week. Everywhere I look, there you are." He framed her face with his hands before shifting to push several strands of hair behind her ear. "I want you. And I want to see where this goes. But I know it's a bad time."

"Maybe it's the perfect time."

And as his lips met hers, Bellamy knew she'd never spoken truer words.

It was the perfect time.

DONOVAN PULLED BELLAMY close for a kiss, the motion achingly beautiful. Hadn't he dreamed of doing this for the past week? Every time he looked at her, he imagined her in his arms. He saw himself peeling off her clothing, piece by piece, until there was nothing between them. And then, once they were both naked, satisfying this hunger that had gripped him and refused to let go.

She'd been so brave. He saw the toll the sitting and

waiting had taken, yet she'd remained hopeful. Focused on the future and their ability to find whoever was behind the attacks on her. It had only been today, after she'd finished up on the computer, that he'd finally seen the cracks.

And he had more than a few cracks of his own.

He wanted her. He knew there were consequences to taking this leap but heaven help him, he couldn't walk away.

"Donovan?"

"Hmm?" He kissed her again.

"Stop thinking and take me to bed."

He lifted his head then and stared down at her, a seductive smile lighting her up from the inside. "You're sure?"

"I've never been more sure. I want you. And I want to make love with you. Let's take what's between us and not worry about anything else."

Had he ever met anyone so generous? Or wanted a woman more?

All the questions that had swirled around his life for the past week—heck, for the past thirty-one years—seemed to fade in the face of her. She was warm and generous and she took him as he was. That was a gift beyond measure and he swore to himself he wouldn't squander it.

Her home was small and he was grateful for that when they arrived at her bedroom a short while later. They'd stripped each other along the way, a path of shirts and pants and a sexy bra forming a trail from the kitchen to the bedroom. And after he laid her down on the bed, her arms extending to pull him close, he sank into her, reveling in the play of skin against skin, the full press of her breasts against his chest a delicious torment.

Slipping a hand between them, he found the waistband of her panties, the last piece of clothing to come off. The warm heat of her covered his hand and he played with her sensitive flesh, gratified by the sexy moans that spilled from her throat and the gentle writhing of her legs where they pressed to his hips. She was amazing. Warm. Responsive. And as in the moment as he was.

Long, glorious moments spun out between them as the dying afternoon light spilled into the room. They had all they needed there, just the two of them, as their touches grew more urgent. As fewer words were exchanged. As soft sighs expanded, growing longer before cresting on a gentle breath.

They didn't need anything else, Donovan realized as he jumped up on a rush and raced for his discarded jeans. Her light giggle had followed him out of the room as he ran for protection and her smile was pure and golden when she opened her arms for him and welcomed him back to the bed.

Welcome.

The thought struck hard as he rejoined her, making quick work of the condom before fitting himself to her body.

She was the warmest, softest welcome and it nearly killed him to go slow and take his time. To make the moments last between the two of them, as powerful as a tornado, as delicate as spun sugar.

The demands of her body pulled against him as he moved inside of her, her delicate inner walls indicating her release was nearly upon her. He added a firm touch to pull her along, gratified when she crested mere moments before he followed her.

Pure pleasure suffused his body as he wrapped himself up in her. And as he rode out wave after wave, he knew nothing in his life would ever be the same.

Bellamy had changed him.

And he had no desire to go back to the way he'd been.

JENSEN FITTED THE small hunting cabin at the edge of the LSP property with a strip of explosive. He fashioned the claylike material around the needed wires and then worked backward toward the detonation device.

His father had kept this place, private land adjacent to LSP, as a small getaway right in the heart of the Hill Country. How apropos that a place used to destroy God's creatures had become a human hunting ground, as well.

He'd waited for this, carefully mapping out how he'd secure Bellamy Reeves's arrival at the cabin. In the end, he had no idea it would be so easy as snatching her sister as an incentive to come without a fuss.

Maggie Corgan was hot, but damn, the woman was a sad sack. She'd been moping around Whisperwood like a bored prom queen and it had been easy enough to grab her and bring her here. He'd made a point to run into her in town and made a fuss about some details they'd found at LSP on Bellamy's car. Despite the holiday, the woman had practically jumped into his passenger seat, anxious to find the details that would exonerate her sister.

The chloroformed cloth had knocked her out just

after they passed the gated entrance to LSP property and she'd been asleep ever since.

"Do you know what you're doing?" Sally's voice echoed from the small front room slash kitchen, her tone growing increasingly naggy and whiny as they got closer to finishing this. He'd seriously misjudged her. He thought he had a partner in his efforts to secure his future—and he was paying her off well enough for that partnership—but she'd gotten increasingly worried over the past few days. She wouldn't stop asking him if he knew how to handle things and she was convinced his old man was going to make a magical recovery from his blood poisoning.

What good was it to own a pharmaceutical company if you couldn't co-op a few of the products for your own use? The chloroform fell into that category. So did the experimental drug he'd used on his father. That had been the easy part.

Setting up Bellamy Reeves to take the fall while he initiated his "brother" Donovan into the family? Now that took real planning.

"It's fine, Sally. I've got it all under control."

"You said that a week ago and since then I've fielded daily calls from the police nosing around. You're lucky I know my rights. They can't get in without a search warrant and so far they can't get one."

"Good."

"So far, Jensen. It's only a matter of time if I keep blocking."

"The problem will be gone by then and you'll be long gone. Calm down."

She gave him a side-eye but marched back into the front room. He was glad to see her go. The nagging was driving him crazy. They said men looked for women like their mothers, and in that respect he had to agree. His mother might have been a passive soul, but she knew her place and didn't harp and harangue every chance she got.

No, Jensen thought with no small measure of glee. *His* mother had taken notes. Detailed notes she'd left behind for him to find and pore over. She'd not mentioned Donovan Colton by name but it had been easy enough to note the Christmas date and the reference to Sutton's latest "bastard left in the stables across town like a discarded piece of trash."

He'd read that passage more than once, pleased to know his father was oblivious to the brat's existence. It would make it that much easier to ensure Donovan Colton never got a piece of the Taylor inheritance.

Jensen snipped an extra length of wire and tested the hold. It was only a matter of time until Bellamy Reeves showed up, her knight in shining armor in tow.

And then Donovan Colton would understand, once and for all, what a discarded piece of trash he really was.

DONOVAN LEVERED HIS hands behind his head and watched as Bellamy flitted around the room. She was full of nervous energy post-sex that he found incredibly adorable and he was enjoying just watching her. Especially since he felt like every muscle in his body had just had the best, most effective workout. It was a treat to lay back and watch her beautiful frame and whip-quick energy light up the room.

"Maybe I should have gotten a tree? I know I didn't

want one, but it'd have been nice to have the color. And the smell. I love that fresh tree smell."

"We can still get one if you'd like one."

She stopped midpace, a hand going to her hip. "You wouldn't mind doing that?"

"Not at all. Let's do it."

She glanced own, her eyes widening. "But we're naked."

"So we'll get dressed and then get naked later."

"Later?"

He smiled at the slight squeak in her voice. "I'd like that, if you would."

Bellamy crossed to the bed, her nervous energy fading as a soft smile spread across her face. "I'd like that, too. Even as crazy and scary as this time has been, I wouldn't change it."

"Me, either." Donovan reached for her and pulled her close, nestling her against his chest. "Not one single second."

She pressed her lips against his skin before lifting her head. "I'm glad you're here."

"Me, too." He tickled her before rolling her over on her back. "Let's go buy a tree."

"Now?"

"Maybe in an hour."

And then he proceeded to show her just what he could do with an hour.

BELLAMY PRACTICALLY DANCED through the kitchen, gathering up her purse and her phone where they still lay on the counter. She couldn't believe what a difference an afternoon could make in her spirits and her attitude.

She'd spent the morning morose and frustrated and had spent the afternoon in Donovan's arms.

And what an amazing afternoon it had been.

Catching herself before a sigh escaped her lips and already imagining the cartoon hearts that were floating above her head, she took her phone firmly in hand and hit the home screen out of habit. A text from her sister showed up, followed by a phone number she didn't recognize, along with a voice mail prompt.

She'd been waiting for insurance to call her back about her car and had to catch herself a good ten seconds into the voice mail before she realized the message wasn't from her insurance company at all.

A muffled voice, disguised with some sort of filter, echoed against her ear. "Come to the LSP grounds alone if you want to bring your sister home."

She fumbled the phone and listened to the message once more, a desperate sense of urgency forcing her into action, as the message also outlined an appointed time and meeting place. She had to leave. She had to get to Maggie.

Why hadn't she tried harder to talk to her this week? Instead of being persistent and trying to win her sister back, all she'd done was curl into her usual shell and get angry. It was always someone else's fault. She was never the one to blame.

And where had it gotten her?

With Maggie's life in danger, all because of her.

Donovan's voice rumbled from the hallway, where he talked to Alex, and Bellamy quickly cataloged what to do. Tell him where she was going and put Maggie's life at risk? Or take his car and go alone?

This was about her. For reasons she still didn't understand, she'd been targeted by someone inside LSP and all that had ensued was directed at her.

She needed to be the one to fix it.

Her hand closed over Donovan's keys, where they lay on the counter near her purse. She had them in hand, their heft and weight firm in her palm. She would do this. She'd face this nameless threat and handle it. She had to.

The door beckoned but Bellamy stilled, her resolve wavering.

She *could* do this. She could do anything she set her mind to.

But she could also use the help. Qualified help from an expert trained in crisis and criminal behavior.

"Donovan!" He and Alex came running the moment she screamed.

And as man and dog rounded the corner into her kitchen, Bellamy took solace that she'd not have to act alone.

THE NERVOUS ENERGY that had carried her from the house to the drive to the far end of LSP's property faded as Bellamy caught sight of Sally Borne in the distance. "She's behind all this?"

Bellamy supposed it wasn't all that big a revelation, yet somehow she hadn't seen Sally at the heart of everything. A lackey, maybe, taking orders from the inside, but not as a mastermind behind what had happened to her or the decision to throttle drug production.

The disguised tones on her voice mail hadn't suggested a woman, either, yet Bellamy couldn't argue with the tall, feminine form traipsing and tromping around outside the small hideaway bordering the edge of the LSP property. It was a hunting cabin, as she recalled. Something Sutton Taylor had used for years as a place to let off steam on the weekends.

"She looks mad," Donovan whispered in her ear as he lowered night vision goggles. "A plan unraveling?"

"Or a crazy person at the end of her rope."

"That, too." Donovan took her hand in his and squeezed. "We'll take her down and we'll get Maggie back."

"You seem awfully sure about this."

"It's my job to be sure. It's also my job to pin criminals in their dens so we can haul them in."

His certainty helped, as did the knowledge that he had been through something like this before. All she could think of was that Maggie was inside the cabin, but Donovan had a broader purview. He knew how to manage an op and he also knew how to take down a criminal.

And he also had backup setting themselves up in the distance. The two of them hadn't walked into this alone, despite the clear warning on the voice mail to do so.

She'd trusted Donovan to do the right thing, but knew it wasn't going to be easy. They'd gotten in but they still needed to get out.

"I don't believe it's Sally. She was unpleasant and dismissed me from the company without giving me the opportunity to defend myself, but I didn't take her for a kidnapper and a killer."

"Maybe she got in over her head," Donovan suggested.

"Or maybe you did." The voice was low and quiet in the winter night, but the click of a cocked gun was unmistakable.

How HAD HE allowed himself to get so distracted?

That thought pounded through Donovan's mind as he covered the remaining ground from the LSP property to the cabin in the woods. He was responsible for keeping Bellamy safe and there was no way he could do that with a loaded gun at his back.

He hadn't seen his assailant's face, but had to give Bellamy points for gut instinct. She couldn't believe Sally Borne was responsible for what had unfolded, and she wasn't. Sally was in this up to her eyeballs, but she wasn't the mastermind.

Donovan toyed with turning on his assailant, but the proximity made it nearly impossible to get an upper hand. If he was by himself, he'd make the move and worry about any possible consequences in the fight, but with Bellamy by his side, it put her at too much risk. Which only reinforced why she belonged home in the first place.

He'd done his best to convince her to stay behind, but nothing had swayed her.

Including the promise that he'd bring Maggie home.

So he'd listened and believed they could keep her safe anyway, buying into her BS that LSP would only negotiate with her. He'd trusted that Archer and his backup fanning the perimeter would be enough and that he could keep her safe, no matter what.

Now he wasn't so sure.

"Come in, come in." The gun pressed to his back as the jerk marching behind them pushed them inside the front door of the cabin. "We're going to have a family reunion."

Bellamy had stiffened each time the man behind them spoke, but it was only once they were inside the door that she whirled on him. "Jensen Taylor. You're behind all of this?"

Jensen?

Donovan's mind raced over his memories of Jensen Taylor. The paunchy man before him was a genuine surprise and he realized that any of the articles he'd read on the father had limited information about the son.

And old pictures.

Taylor had been a popular, good-looking guy, more than able to get his fair share of dates. But the man that stared back at them had changed. The degree of crazy in his eyes was concerning, but it was something more. He was in his midthirties, but he was already soft, his body doughy and neglected. If it weren't for the gun and Bellamy's close presence, Donovan would have immediately taken his chance at overpowering the man.

"Who were you expecting?" Jensen sneered.

Bellamy shook her head. "I'm not sure but certainly not the heir to the company."

"That's exactly why I'm involved," Jensen said. "I need to make sure I stay that way."

"Stay what way? You're Sutton's son. You already sit in on board meetings and you've got a big position inside LSP."

"It's not big enough. Nor is running distribution a sign that I'm being groomed for the CEO's spot. I decided I need to set up my own plan for upward mobility."

"So you fixed the prices of vaccines?" Bellamy practically spat out the words, her gray eyes nearly black in the soft lighting of the room. "And then tried to blame it on me."

"I did blame it on you. It's just my luck that my little brother over here showed up to play knight in shining armor. He kept rescuing you instead of letting you take the fall."

"Your brother?" Bellamy whispered, her gaze colliding with Donovan's. He saw the awareness there and the subtle agreement that he'd been right with his theory about Sutton Taylor's infidelities.

The question was, how did they all get out of there before his big brother imploded?

BELLAMY KEPT HER gaze on Maggie, willing her sister to wake up. She was tied to a chair, her head lolling at a strange angle from where she'd been knocked out. She wanted to go to her, but Jensen's insistence on keeping the gun cocked and pointed directly at her and Donovan had her staying in place.

They needed to talk him down and give Archer enough time to break in.

And they also needed to keep an eye on Sally. The instability that marked Jensen was nowhere in evidence with her. In fact, the more Jensen railed, the calmer Sally got as she stood there, stoically watching the proceedings.

"Why are you so convinced I'm your brother?" Donovan asked the question, his gaze revealing nothing. "I'm a Colton."

"A Colton discovered in the barn on Christmas morning. The whole town knows."

"It's not a secret I was adopted."

"Adopted because you're some stray they felt sorry for."

"Does Sutton know?"

"About you?" A small corner of spittle filled the edge of Jensen's mouth, his skin turning a ripe shade of pink around his collar. "My mother knew about you. A pithy little story, if you must know. Dear old Dad knocked up his secretary. It was my mother who orchestrated everything, convincing your simpering fool of a mother to hand you over to a family who could really take care of you."

"But does Sutton know?" Donovan insisted.

"No. And that's how it's going to stay. My father has already given enough money to his illegitimate offspring. I'm not losing one more piece of my inheritance to the fact he couldn't keep it zipped."

"Fair point." Donovan nodded, his face drawn in sober lines.

Bellamy watched him, fascinated as he began to subtly control the room. She could only assume he'd received some signal from the chief, because bit by bit, he maneuvered Jensen around the room, drawing the gun off of her and her sister.

"It wouldn't do to have more of your inheritance go to anyone else." Donovan's voice was even and level. Reasonable. "Especially since LSP stock stands to go through the roof with the vaccine price-fixing."

"Exactly."

"You had it all figured out. Work the system, blame it all on Bellamy and then get rid of the evidence."

"Yep." Jensen nodded, the dull red of his skin fading again to a warm pink.

"What about your father?"

"Don't you want to call him Dad?"

It was the first moment Jensen managed to get a rise and the smallest muscle ticked in Donovan's jaw. "Where's Dad in all this?"

"Fighting for his life across town in a quiet little facility that isn't on anyone's radar. He's unknowingly been the recipient of a new drug being developed to treat certain forms of cancer. It's a miracle drug, unless you don't have any cancer to cure."

Bellamy knew what Jensen spoke of and had seen the trial details a few months prior. The drug was powerful and had the potential to be a game changer, but it had to be used properly.

And there he was, poisoning his father with it?

"You're a monster."

"Yeah, sweetheart, I am." Jensen shifted his attention at her outburst, his eyes now wild with whatever madness had gripped him. "But you can take solace in the fact that I'm the last one you're ever going to see."

"You're mad."

"Mad at the world, yes." Jensen's gaze swung toward Donovan before coming firmly to rest on her. "I've spent my life waiting for my turn. To run the company. To earn dear old Dad's respect. To get my shot. Yet I was never good enough."

The roller coaster of the past days seemed to slow in the face of Jensen's anger. It was too simple to think of him as a crazy person to be taken down.

Far too simple.

What she saw instead was a man beyond reason. Whatever he believed was meant to be his—his father's love, his birthright, even the Taylor name—had somehow twisted over time. And as she stared at Jensen, Bellamy had to admit that under different circumstances, that could have been her.

Hadn't she spent the past five years resenting Maggie for choosing to live her life while poor little Bellamy stayed behind taking care of their parents?

And hadn't she buried herself in her job, shunning relationships—heck, even shunning the chance to own a pet—because she'd crawled so far beneath the rock of self-sacrifice?

Looking into Jensen's angry, disillusioned eyes, Bellamy saw it all so clearly. And in that moment, finally understood all she was about to lose.

Donovan and Alex had shown her the way. Even if what was building between her and Donovan still needed time to grow roots, she was grateful for what he'd given her.

For what he'd shown her.

That she had a life and it was time to get living.

How horrifying it was to realize that far too late.

DONOVAN'S FINGERS ITCHED as he held his hands by his side. Brother or not, Jensen Taylor was going down. Assuming he could get them all out of there.

"Nice speech, Jensen."

The words were enough to pull the man's attention off Bellamy and it gave Donovan the briefest moment of relief. If he could keep Jensen's focus diverted, he had a chance of getting Bellamy out alive.

If.

"It's the truth."

"Your truth."

"It is my truth!" Anger spilled from Taylor's lips

with a violence that shouldn't have been surprising under the circumstances. "And now it's yours, Colton. You think you've got a way out of here, but you don't. Even with whatever backup you inevitably brought along, I've thought of it all. This place is wired."

While Donovan didn't doubt Jensen's threats, taunting him might get the information he needed to defuse whatever lurked around the cabin.

"Like Bellamy's car? Because you were so good at that. A half-assed explosion rigged by an amateur."

"It was meant to be. It wasn't time to kill her. And if it gave the cops time to wonder why someone suspected of stealing company secrets would make herself look like an accident victim, it was that much better."

"And the bomb at her house?"

"Same. How does it look if the poor little woman peddling company secrets escaped death twice? It would be like a red flag—she's setting herself up."

"So killing her here? All of us here? How's that going to go down?"

"Ah, that's where Sally comes in. She's the one with Bellamy's personnel folder and she's the one who let her go. It stood to reason the stress of getting discovered and fired was the last thing Bellamy Reeves needed before going around the bend."

"All figured out."

"Except for you," Jensen sneered.

And the backup waiting outside the cabin.

Donovan calculated the odds—and the acknowledgment that Jensen Taylor had to have walked in here with a plan B.

"What are you going to do about me?"

"Same thing I'm going to do about all of you. I came

out here to counsel a distressed former employee. And I'm going to get out barely alive from the bomb she's planted to blow me to smithereens."

Cold. Impersonal. Distant.

The very reason a bomb made an effective weapon for cowards stood before him.

And in that moment, Donovan knew there was no time to wait.

As he leaped forward, Donovan's momentum was enough to knock Jensen off balance. Donovan slammed Jensen's gun hand on the ground, a harsh cry in his ear proof he'd damaged bone, as well. As soon as the man went still, Donovan was on his feet, moving toward Bellamy.

Jensen's fall must have been what Archer was waiting for. The room erupted in gunfire and smoke, a series of officers rushing the room from outside. Donovan had a split second to register it all before Bellamy's scream had his gaze shifting back toward his half brother. The man lifted a small square no bigger than a lighter from his pocket, his hand flipping the top open.

"Donovan!" Bellamy screamed his name once more, just as Donovan leaped into motion. His hand closed over Jensen's, effectively stopping his brother from taking the final step of blowing up the cottage with all of them in it. Archer was the closest, and he twisted Jensen's wrist to retrieve the device that would no doubt blow them all sky-high.

All noise ceased, everyone in the room going quiet as Archer stepped back, the detonation device in hand.

"Tell me you know what you're doing with that, Thompson." Donovan gritted out the words.

"Underestimating me again, Colton?"

"Never."

"Good." Chief Thompson nodded, his hands calm and still. "Then I can swallow my pride and ask you to come handle this."

"Deal."

DONOVAN TAPPED THE back of the EMT vehicle in a signal that the crew could move on. Sally and Jensen had already been transported in handcuffs and the other EMT team had worked on Maggie, treating her for lingering effects of the chloroform and taking her in for an overnight of observation. The bomb beneath the cabin had already been removed, detonated on the far edge of the property where it couldn't hurt anyone. Archer and his men still worked the scene and they'd already called into the facility where Sutton was to get the doctors diagnosing him with the correct meds to get well.

"I had no idea it was Jensen. I never even considered him." That thought had kept her steady company since Archer's team had cuffed Jensen and even an hour later, she still couldn't believe it was true.

Everything that had happened had been engineered by Sutton's greedy—and clearly unstable—son.

"Archer asked me what I thought the motive was in all that was happening."

Bellamy took in his bedraggled form and the spot of blood that had dried on his cheek where Jensen had nicked him in their fight. "What motive did you give?"

"I went with the old standby. Money and power."

"I'd say you pegged them both."

Donovan pulled her close, folding her up against his chest. "I don't know what I'd have done if something happened to you."

He'd said the same thing off and on since Jensen had been taken away, and each time she'd stood patiently, wrapping her arms around his waist and holding him tight. "I'm okay. We all are."

"I never should have let you come."

"You didn't get much choice in the matter."

He shook his head at that, his warm brown gaze still bleak from the events of the evening. "I shouldn't have let that matter."

"Is that how it's going to be, Donovan Colton?"

"Be?"

He looked crestfallen as she pulled from his arms, her own hands fisting at her hips. "You tell me what to do and I just do it. I'm not Alex, you know."

"A fact I'm glad about."

"I have my own mind and I make my own decisions. It's why I stopped and told you what was happening instead of harking off on my own. That was big for me." She moved in and pressed a kiss to his chin. "Don't make me regret my decision."

"Why didn't you leave?"

Bellamy knew there were a lot of reasons she'd chosen to go to Donovan instead of heading out on her own, but one had stood out beyond all the rest. "Because it's time to stick."

"To stick?"

"I've been doing everything on my own for far too long. It's time to depend on people. To let people in and to depend on them and the support they can provide."

"Does this mean you want me to stick around?"

So much had happened in such a short time, it seemed nearly impossible to be having this conversation.

Yet here they were.

She'd spent too much time unwilling to voice what she wanted, now that the moment was here, Bellamy was determined not to fumble it. "Yes, I do."

"I'm not in a position to walk away from my job in Austin."

"I'd never ask you to."

"And Alex and I are a package deal."

"I certainly hope so."

"And I'm sort of surly and grumpy in the morning."

She smiled. "Believe it or not, I figured that one out all by myself."

"What else have you figured out?"

"That I want to spend time with you. I like having a surly, grumpy man and his furry best friend in my life. I'm tired of my own company and I'm tired of ignoring all the life going on all around me."

"If you're sure?"

She thought about those scary moments, when she stared at Jensen Taylor and saw the faintest outline of herself.

"I'm absolutely positive."

Donovan bent his head and pressed his lips to hers. The kiss was full of passion and promise and abundant joy. As she wrapped her arms around him and sunk into his kiss, Bellamy knew she'd finally found the partner to share her life with.

Two partners, she silently acknowledged to herself as she added Alex. And she couldn't be happier.

Epilogue

Six weeks later

Bellamy juggled the plate of cake and pot of coffee and headed for the living room. She'd come to look forward to these Saturday afternoons with her sister and was excited to share the recently discovered recipe with Maggie.

"Is that Mom's pound cake?" The words were said in a reverent tone as Maggie leaped off the couch to help her with the plate.

"I found the recipe back in the fall. She had it hoarded in the bottom of her jewelry box."

"Who knew?" Maggie's musical laughter was a balm and Bellamy couldn't deny how nice it was to share something funny about her parents.

"She was so proud of that cake. She preened every time someone commented on it at town events."

Maggie reached for a slice. "Then I'm glad it's not lost to us."

Her sister took a bite, her eyes closing as she chewed, and Bellamy screwed up her courage. She'd wanted to say something for a while now, but had struggled with how to express all she felt. "I'm sorry for all that's happened."

Maggie's eyes popped open. "What do you mean?"

"Mom. Dad. All of it. I was stubborn and unfair to you and I'm sorry. I'm sorrier it took a kidnapping and an attempt on both our lives to realize it."

"I'm sorry, too."

"You don't have to be sorry."

"Yes, actually, I do." Maggie settled her plate back on the coffee table. "I thought I could fix everything. That marrying James would give me the financial tools to fix what was happening. I'm not proud of myself, nor was I fair to James."

"But you loved him first."

"Yes. Maybe." Maggie swiped at a small tear that trailed down her cheek. "It's the 'maybe' that's the problem. For a long time, I enjoyed being with him. And I liked being a Corgan. But I liked those things too much. My husband should have come first."

Since coming back into each other's lives, she and Maggie had danced around the subject of her sister's marriage. It was humbling to realize all that had gone on beneath the surface. "But you did care for each other."

"We did. And I'm glad we finally remembered that, there at the end. But James has moved on and in time, I will, too. And in the meantime, he helped me make sure you've got this great house."

"He… You what?"

A mischievous light filled Maggie's eyes. "You belong here, Bell. And I know it's what Mom and Dad would have wanted."

"But the will. The insurance. The house came from there—" Bellamy broke off. "Didn't it?"

"They actually came courtesy of the Corgan fortune."

A sinking feeling gripped her, and Bellamy felt the coffee she'd sipped curdling in her stomach. "I can't accept that. I mean, it's not my place."

Maggie reached over, her gentle touch stopping the torrent of words. "It's what James and I both wanted. He understood it was important to me and in a lot of ways, it was the final act of kindness that allowed us to let each other go. And we both decided to keep it a secret so you wouldn't say no."

"But I can't take it."

"Actually, you can. We both knew how much you sacrificed for Mom and Dad. More, you deserved something to cement your future. This is your home."

"But—"

"But nothing. I know you love playing the big-sister card, but on this one, I win. It's what I wanted. James, too."

The generosity was nearly overwhelming, but in her sister's words, Bellamy sensed healing, as well. "You're okay with the divorce?"

"It's best for both of us." Maggie reached for her plate again. "Speaking of best, how are things with Donovan Colton?"

She knew her sister, and Bellamy suspected the rapid change in topic was deliberate. But she also understood how important it was to Maggie to stand on her own two feet. Vowing to take the issue of the house up with her later, she let the joy of being with Donovan wash over her.

"Things are good. He's good."

"You're spending a lot of time running back and forth to Austin."

"We're enjoying each other's company."

"First you make her pound cake and now you're using euphemisms like Mom?"

Bellamy swatted at her sister's leg. "I like being with him."

"Then tell me what you're doing for Valentine's Day."

LATER THAT DAY, her earlier conversation with Maggie still lingered in her mind as Bellamy cleaned up the plates and mugs. The time they'd spent together since the holidays was helping to mend their relationship and it was wonderful to have her sister back.

She heard the bark moments before a nose pressed into her hip, a large, wiggly body prancing at her side. Donovan followed behind Alex into the kitchen and Bellamy fought the urge to lay a hand against her heart at the sight of him. She bent to lavish praise on Alex instead, willing her pulse to slow down.

How did the man manage it?

"Where's Maggie?"

"She had a date with a sale at the mall."

He moved in and pulled her close. "And you didn't want to go?"

"I'm getting used to having some money back in my bank account. I'd like to revel in that glow a bit longer."

Concern lined his face. "Sutton's made good on everything that happened at LSP. Your job, your good name *and* a raise."

She wrapped her arms around his waist, unable to hold back the truth. "Okay. I admit it, then. I wanted to stay home and spend the afternoon with you."

The worry faded, replaced with a cocky smile. "Well, then, Ms. Reeves. What did you have in mind?"

"This."

The kiss had her pulse racing again, a wild thrill ride that she couldn't imagine ever tiring of.

How things had changed since December. Her lonely, quiet life had vanished and in its place was something more wonderful than she could have ever imagined.

She was in love.

The thought hit so swiftly—and came from a place so deep—it had Bellamy pulling back from the kiss.

Love?

"Bellamy?"

"I... Um... I..." She grasped at the first thing that came to mind. "Do we need to feed Alex?"

"What?" Confusion furrowed a small line between his eyebrows before Donovan glanced toward Alex, who even now lay curled up on the floor, fast asleep. "He's fine."

"Good."

"And he doesn't eat until six."

"Right."

"It's one."

"Sure." Bellamy silently cursed herself for her inability to think on the fly. "Of course."

"Are you okay?"

"Yeah. Sure. I'm fine." She moved back to the sink and snatching up a dish towel to dry the mugs from earlier.

"What's wrong?"

"Nothing."

"Something's wrong. One moment I'm kissing you and the next you're pulling away like you got burned. What's wrong?"

She dropped the dish towel as the cup banged against the counter with a discordant thud. "I love you."

The words were out before she could check them and it was enough to have her holding her breath. Had she really just told him she loved him?

It was stupid and impulsive and about as well thought out as the "let's feed Alex" line.

"Bellamy."

The second, urgent use of her name had her looking up, turning to face him. To face the reality of her impulsive words. "Look. Just ignore me. That kiss scrambled my brain and I sort of short-circuited. It's noth—"

He laid a finger over her lips. "It's not nothing."

The soft press of his finger turned tantalizing as he ran the pad over her lower lip. "Believe it or not, I have a few thoughts on this subject you seem hesitant to voice, too. It's not particularly original but I think it fits in these circumstances."

"You do?"

"I love you, Bellamy Reeves. I love everything about you. I love that you don't mind my attitude in the morning before coffee. And I love that you've been quietly encouraging me to visit with Sutton *and* my parents. And I love that you're mending fences with your sister."

"Those are good things."

"They are. And they're good because I can share them with you."

Whatever she'd been expecting, a declaration of love was the farthest thing from her mind. "You love me back?"

"I sure do."

"I love you, Donovan. And I love your furry partner, too."

"Alex is a lot smarter than me. I think he already figured it all out and has been waiting for the two humans to get on board."

The heavy thump of a tail had the two of them turning at the same time. The sleeping lump in front of her fridge was wide-awake, his dark eyes full of knowing and endless wisdom.

Bellamy smiled, surprised at how easy it was to believe the dog knew all. "I guess that means he approves."

As if on cue, Alex leaped up from his favorite spot and jumped up, completing the small circle in Bellamy's kitchen and pressing eager kisses on both of them.

Bellamy laughed as Donovan tightened his hold.

"Oh yeah," Donovan whispered against her ear. "He definitely approves."

* * * * *

If you loved this suspenseful story,
don't miss these previous books in the
COLTONS OF SHADOW CREEK *miniseries:*

THE BILLIONAIRE'S COLTON THREAT
by Geri Krotow
MISSION: COLTON JUSTICE
by Jennifer Morey
CAPTURING A COLTON
by C.J. Miller
THE COLTON MARINE
by Lisa Childs
COLD CASE COLTON
by Addison Fox
PREGNANT BY THE COLTON COWBOY
by Lara Lacombe
COLTON UNDERCOVER
by Marie Ferrarella
COLTON'S SECRET SON
by Carla Cassidy

All available now from
Harlequin Romantic Suspense.

I N T R I G U E

Available November 21, 2017

#1749 ALWAYS A LAWMAN
Blue River Ranch • by Delores Fossen
Years ago, Jodi Canton and Sheriff Gabriel Beckett were torn apart by a shocking murder and false conviction. Can they now face the true killer and rekindle the love they thought they'd lost?

#1750 REDEMPTION AT HAWK'S LANDING
Badge of Justice • by Rita Herron
The murder of her father has brought Honey Granger back to her small Texas town, but despite his attraction to Honey the hot Sheriff Harrison Hawk has his own motives for looking into her father's death—the disappearance of his sister.

#1751 MILITARY GRADE MISTLETOE
The Precinct • by Julie Miller
Master Sergeant Harry Lockheart was the only survivor of the IED that killed his team—but he credits Daisy Gunderson's kind letters to his actual recovery. And now that he's finally met the woman of his dreams, he's not about to let a stalker destroy their dreams for the future.

#1752 PROTECTOR'S INSTINCT
Omega Sector: Under Siege • by Janie Crouch
When former police detective Zane Wales couldn't protect Caroline Gill, he left both her and the force behind, unable to face his failure. But now that a psychopath has Caroline in his sights, can Zane find the courage to face the past and protect the woman he loves still?

#1753 MS. DEMEANOR
Mystery Christmas • by Danica Winters
Rainier Fitzgerald manages to attract both a heap of trouble and the attention of his parole officer, Laura Blade, only hours after his release. Can the two of them crack the cold case on Dunrovin ranch or will Christmas be behind bars?

#1754 THE DEPUTY'S WITNESS
The Protectors of Riker County • by Tyler Anne Snell
Testifying against a trio of lethal bank robbers has drawn a target on Alyssa Garner's back, and the only man who can save her from the crosshairs is cop Caleb Foster, who harbors secrets of his own...

YOU CAN FIND MORE INFORMATION ON UPCOMING HARLEQUIN® TITLES, FREE EXCERPTS AND MORE AT WWW.HARLEQUIN.COM.

HICNM1117

Get 2 Free Books,
Plus 2 Free Gifts—
just for trying the Reader Service!

SPECIAL EXCERPT FROM

◆ **HARLEQUIN**®

I N T R I G U E

Years ago, Jodi Canton and Sheriff Gabriel Beckett
were torn apart by a shocking murder and false
conviction. Can they now face the true killer and
rekindle the love they thought they'd lost?

Read on for a sneak preview of
ALWAYS A LAWMAN,
*the first book in the **BLUE RIVER RANCH** series from*
New York Times *bestselling author Delores Fossen!*

She had died here. Temporarily, anyway.

But she was alive now, and Jodi Canton could feel the nerves just beneath the surface of her skin. With the Smith & Wesson gripped in her hand, she inched closer to the dump site where he had left her for dead.

There were no signs of the site now. Nearly ten years had passed, and the thick Texas woods had reclaimed the ground. It didn't look nearly so sinister dotted with wildflowers and a honeysuckle vine coiling over it. No drag marks.

No blood.

The years had washed it all away, but Jodi could see it, smell it and even taste it as if it were that sweltering July night when a killer had come within a breath of ending her life.

The nearby house had succumbed to time and the elements, too. It'd been a home then. Now the white paint was blistered, several of the windows on the bottom floor closed off with boards that had grayed with age. Of course, she hadn't expected this place to ever feel like anything but the crime scene that it had once been.

Considering that two people had been murdered inside.

Jodi adjusted the grip on the gun when she heard the footsteps. They weren't hurried, but her visitor wasn't trying to sneak up on her, either. Jodi had been listening for that. Listening for everything that could get her killed.

Permanently this time.

Just in case she was wrong about who this might be, Jodi pivoted and took aim at him.

"You shouldn't have come here," he said. His voice was husky and deep, part lawman's growl, part Texas drawl.

The man was exactly who she thought it might be. Sheriff Gabriel Beckett. No surprise that he had arrived, since this was Beckett land, and she'd parked in plain sight on the side of the road that led to the house. Even though the Becketts no longer lived here, Gabriel would have likely used the road to get to his current house.

"You came," Jodi answered, and she lowered her gun.

Muttering some profanity with that husky drawl, Gabriel walked to her side, his attention on the same area where hers was fixed. Or at least it was until he looked at her the same exact moment that she looked at him.

Their gazes connected.

And now it was Jodi who wanted to curse. Really? After all this time that punch of attraction was still there? She had huge reasons for the attraction to go away and not a single reason for it to stay.

Yet it remained.

Don't miss
ALWAYS A LAWMAN,
available December 2017 wherever
Harlequin® Intrigue books and ebooks are sold.

www.Harlequin.com

HIEXP1117

THE WORLD IS BETTER WITH

Romance

Harlequin has everything from contemporary, passionate and heartwarming to suspenseful and inspirational stories.

Whatever your mood, we have a romance just for you!

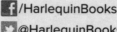